2.

James Pattinson is a full-time author who, despite having travelled throughout the world, still lives in the remote village where he grew up. He has written magazine articles, short stories and radio features as well as numerous novels, including his last, *Crane*.

THE SILENT VOYAGE

World War Two has ended a few years earlier and the Cold War is starting when Brett Manning is sent to do some business in Archangel. But on his way, in the thick fog and darkness of the Barents Sea, his ship is run down by a much larger vessel. Only Brett and one other man are picked up, and they now find themselves on board a Russian freighter bound for a secret destination. Slowly it dawns on Brett and his companion that they now know too much for their own good and that their very lives are in danger. But how does one escape from a ship at sea?

JAMES PATTINSON

THE SILENT VOYAGE

Complete and Unabridged

ULVERSCROFT
Leicester

First published in Great Britain in 1958 as
'The Mystery of the 'Gregory Kotovsky''

First Large Print Edition
published 2003
by arrangement with
Robert Hale Limited
London

British Library CIP Data

Pattinson, James
    The silent voyage.—Large print ed.—
    Ulverscroft large print series: adventure & suspense
    1. Suspense fiction
    2. Large type books
    I. Title II. The mystery of the Gregory Kotovsky
    823.9'14 [F]

    ISBN 0–7089–4818–9

Published by
F. A. Thorpe (Publishing)
Anstey, Leicestershire

Set by Words & Graphics Ltd.
Anstey, Leicestershire
Printed and bound in Great Britain by
T. J. International Ltd., Padstow, Cornwall

This book is printed on acid-free paper

Prologue

Grinkov's Tomb is an island. That is, if such a term can rightly be applied to what is in fact no more than a bare rock, lifting its forbidding head above those icy waters that stretch like a girdle round the bleak Antarctic continent. No vegetation grows on it; no animal makes a home there. It is chilled by bitter winds, frequently veiled in fog, and beaten upon by great waves. It is an outpost of land in a desert of sea, offering no comfort to the sailor and no hope to the castaway.

The man from whom the island takes its name was an obscure Russian seaman, Vladimir Grinkov, who in the year 1834 found himself serving in a New England whaler, the *Cyrus Brilling* of Nantucket.

This vessel having been at sea for many months, without profit, and with much ill fortune, it fell to Grinkov's lot, being a foreigner, to be blamed for all the evil luck that had befallen the ship. Indeed, so convinced were the crew that he was a Jonah that when they found themselves being driven on to an uncharted rock in the lonely waters of the Southern Ocean they took the law into

1

their own hands and cast him into the sea.

That the ship was not thereafter wrecked, but managed to claw off the lee shore on which it had appeared doomed to be broken up, was attributed by the sailors entirely to their timely action in ridding themselves of the disastrous Russian. That they afterwards sighted whales in good number, and returned safely to Nantucket with a full and lucrative cargo of sperm-oil, was considered further proof of the rightness of their action. They were no doubt surprised to find that a court of law, sitting in judgment on them, should have taken a different view, and that in consequence some of them should have been compelled to serve a term in gaol.

This punishment of his murderers did not, however, bring back to life poor Vladimir Grinkov, and it would perhaps have been small consolation to him in his hour of bitter anguish had he known that his name was to be for ever graven upon a monument more awe-inspiring and imposing than any marble tombstone or gilded tablet.

Nevertheless, he is no longer alone in his grave. Ten years later a whaler was wrecked on the jagged reef which extends westward from the rock, and all her crew perished. Soon after another whaler, the Norwegian vessel *Trondhjem*, ran on to the reef in thick weather, and only one man was rescued at considerable risk by a sister ship.

From time to time other sailing ships suffered a similar dismal fate, and gradually superstition grew up around the island. Seamen maintained that it was haunted by the ghost of Grinkov; that the unfortunate Russian now lured ships on to the reef by arts, known only to the dead, in order that others might be forced to share his lonely resting-place.

Superstition or not, it was fully believed — not only by ignorant seamen but by ships' captains also, and no other argument was needed to persuade them to keep far away from those rocky and inhospitable shores.

Grinkov's Tomb was never an important island, and was too small to be marked on any ordinary map of the world. Even its name was unknown to any but seamen; and to them it had only an evil reputation. But in 1952 it burst suddenly into prominence, in a manner of which poor Vladimir Grinkov could never have dreamed.

1

Manning and Company

It was mid-October, a chilly day even though the sun was shining, a day to suggest that winter was not far away. A wind, coming in from the sea, and blowing, cold and blustery, up the harbour, rippled the dark surface of the river and made the ships, huddling against the quays on either side, stir uneasily and tug gently at their mooring-ropes, as though testing the strength of these ties which bound them to the land.

They were not great ships — not mammoth liners or vast tankers, capable of transporting five million gallons of oil; for such vessels did not, and indeed could not, use this east coast port, famous more for its fishing-fleet than for its international trade. And the ships that did come came mostly from the east — from Northern Europe, from Scandinavia, from Finland, and from Russia, moving to and fro across the North Sea with cargoes as various as the house flags painted on their smoky funnels. Of one particular kind of cargo that they brought there was evidence in the big, open-sided sheds on the right bank of the river, sheds piled high with timber. There were planks of every conceivable length and thickness, mounting towards the roofs in stacks that were straight and sheer as a cliff at one end, while at the other they climbed in irregular steps, the longer planks poking out beyond the shorter.

In the lee of one of these timber stores, apparently sheltering behind it from the chilly wind, was a long, low wooden building, with a corrugated iron roof painted a dull and depressing maroon. Along the ridge of this roof was fixed a vertical board some two feet in width, with a serrated upper edge like that of a giant saw. The board was black, and on it was painted in large white letters the legend: Josiah Manning, Son, and Company, Limited. Timber Importers. Registered Office.

On this particular October day in the year 1951 the 'Son' of Josiah Manning, Son, and Co, Ltd, was sitting behind his desk in a small but comfortably furnished room at one end of the long building, and smoking a cigar. Josiah Manning himself had been dead for twenty years, and Robertson Manning, the son, was well past his sixtieth year. He was a stocky, broad shouldered man with a hard, angular face and iron-grey hair cropped very close to the head. His hands, now folded over

6

the solid gold watch-chain which hung in two loops on either side of his waistcoat buttons, were large and bony, with thick, scarred fingers and prominent veins. It was one of Robertson's favourite boasts that he had started at the bottom, working as a labourer in his father's timber yard before progressing to a place in the office and a desk of his own. That was Josiah's method of training.

'Know the job from A to Z,' Robertson would say. 'It's the best way, too. If you don't know what the job is, how can you give orders? I never was afraid of hard work and I'll have nobody in my employ who is.'

Even now he would often go out among the workmen and carry baulks of timber, not because it was necessary for him to do so, but because he liked to show that he could if he wished, that even at his age he was still fit and strong and not afraid — as he put it — to dirty his hands.

'Pen-pushing — that's no job for a man. We have to do it, more's the pity; but it's not a man's job, devil take it!' The autumn sunshine, peering in through the dusty window at his back, glinted on his hair and imparted a certain glow, a certain warmth, to the craggy head. He took the cigar from his mouth and shifted to a more comfortable position in his chair.

'I'm glad to have you back in the business, Brett; I won't deny it. Not that I'm not fit for years of work yet, mind you; and not that I couldn't carry on single-handed if it comes to that. But I shan't live for ever; no man can do that; and it's you who'll have to take over where I leave off. So I'm glad you're back and ready to get down to things. Damn nuisance, this National Service, taking a boy just when he's beginning to be useful. Though I dare say it's good for you — discipline, travel, and all that. I suppose they taught you a few things, hey?'

'Oh yes, quite a few things, Uncle.'

'Spit and polish, marching, rifle drill — that sort of damned nonsense.'

'And the best method of sticking a bayonet into people.'

'Oh — ah — yes — no doubt. Not much call for that in this business, though.'

'No; but you never know when it might come in useful.'

Brett Manning, seated opposite his uncle on the other side of the desk, showed a certain family likeness to the older man. He was taller, but there was the same impression of latent strength in the shoulders, the same thick body, the same bony formation of the face, the straight mouth, the shrewd, assessing expression of the grey eyes, as

8

though they were peering, not at a man's outward shell, but into his heart, his mind, trying to read his inmost thoughts.

The Mannings had always been a clear-sighted family. 'We can see as far into a brick wall as the next man,' Robertson would say. 'And a damn lot farther than most.' They had also been keen men of business — business first and play a very poor second. Indeed, Robertson had never been known to play a game of any sort since the day he left school and became, in his own estimation, a man. 'None of that kids' stuff any more. Men amusing themselves with things like that! It's just plain daft.' To Robertson life was real, life was earnest, and only a fool played about with it.

Brett did not entirely agree. He enjoyed football and cricket and tennis. He did not make them his gods; he did not worship them; but in their proper place, their correct perspective, he felt that they were all very well. He liked boxing, too, and of this Robertson did not altogether disapprove. Ball games — there was no sense in them; but boxing could not truly be classed as a game; it was the art of self-defence, the noble art, and you never knew when it might come in useful. A man ought to know how to use his fists.

Brett's hair was longer than his uncle's, though not long enough to attract Robertson's disapproval. Raven black and rather stiff, it was not a willing slave to brush and comb; as a rule it had a wind-swept, untidy appearance. If his face had been less angular and bony Brett might have been handsome; and then Robertson would probably have despised him, for if there was one thing he could not stand it was a pretty face on a man's shoulders. 'If a man's a man he ought to look like one, not like a blasted female dressed up in trousers. Damn me if you can tell the difference half the time these days. God knows what things are coming to.'

Brett, who had received his name from his mother's side of the family, might well have inherited other legacies that would have disgusted his uncle. The Bretts — those damned Bretts, as Robertson called them — were inclined to be artistic. They loved, and discussed, music, literature, painting, sculpture, ballet — all things which the rugged timber merchant regarded with a stout and proper contempt. 'Thank God the young 'un takes after our family. That woman was never the right wife for George — her and her highfalutin talk about Picasso and Matisse and all the rest of them. I told him so at the time, but he wouldn't listen; always was headstrong, George. But I was right. Look what happened.'

What had happened was that Penelope had dragged George Manning off to Italy to see the art treasures of that country and to listen to opera in its spiritual home. In Milan they had both been killed in a motor accident, and Robertson felt ever afterwards that the entire Brett family, with their damned long-haired nonsense, were directly responsible for the loss of his only brother.

There was one compensation: he became guardian of the boy; and as his own three children were all girls he looked upon Brett as a son and watched him grow to manhood with a keen and critical eye for any evidence of those weaknesses that might have been handed down from the mother's side. To his profound relief he had detected none, except perhaps a love of reading; and even that could not be held too much against the lad, since it was good virile stuff that he read — the *Boys' Own paper*, Henty, Stevenson, Kipling, and Westerman — no erotic nonsense, no effeminate poetry, only fine, rollicking verses like *The Ballad of East and West or The Ingoldsby Legends*.

For the rest, Brett grew up just as he would have wished a son to grow — strong, athletic, hard-muscled. 'He's a Manning,' Robertson would say gleefully. 'He's a Manning, every inch of him. What could you expect? The Manning blood was too strong for that weak liquid his mother had in her veins. But it was a risk, all the same; a hell of a risk.' He spoke as though his brother's marriage had been some hazardous business investment which might well have been a complete loss but fortunately was not.

Brett himself did not altogether share Robertson's views of his mother's family. He found them cheerful, friendly people, with far wider interests than those of the old timber merchant, whose whole existence seemed to be bound up in the business of buying and selling. The Bretts might not make vast sums of money — they were far too unmaterialistic for that — but they knew how to live, and from them young Brett derived a healthy antidote to his uncle's rather too restricted outlook.

Robertson puffed at his cigar and gazed at his nephew. Army life had done the lad no harm, it seemed. He had filled out, no longer looked such a kid; and no doubt he'd learnt a thing or two during the last couple of years. What was it he'd been in? Intelligence! Must have had brains for that, surely. Well, it was all right to have brains, so long as you used them for the right purpose.

'I believe you learned to speak Russian.'

'Yes,' Brett said. 'There was the chance, and it seemed a good idea.'

'Humph!' Robertson appeared doubtful, as though he felt that the knowledge of a bizarre and outlandish tongue like Russian might be evidence of a strain of maternal weakness showing through. The Russians went in for ballet, didn't they? However, he could not deny the usefulness of the accomplishment.

'You can make them understand, then?'

Brett smiled. 'Reasonably well, I think.'

The Russian language had appealed to him. Its difficulties were a challenge to his mind which he accepted gladly. Deeply interested, he found himself learning with surprising facility, after the initial difficulties had been overcome. He wondered what his uncle was driving at; why he was so interested in this question. Robertson did not leave him long in doubt.

'It's a good thing. I'm sending you to Russia.'

'Sending me?'

'Ay. We're buying a lot of timber from there now, and I thought it would be a good idea if a member of the firm went out to have a look at things. Nothing like the personal contact, you know. I'd go myself if I wasn't needed here; but I'm getting a bit old for that sort of thing, and it'll be an experience for you. Well, what do you say? D'you want to go?'

'Why, of course. It's rather a surprise, though.'

'Never mind that. You're willing to go?'

'Certainly I am; I'd be glad to. When did you propose sending me?'

'The sooner the better. There's a ship discharging right now. She'll be going back to Archangel in a few weeks' time. I've arranged for you to sail with her.'

'You've arranged it? So you expected me to go?'

Robertson chuckled. 'You wouldn't have been a nephew of mine if you hadn't jumped at the chance. The formalities are nearly complete. It's not everybody who can get into the country these days, but it makes a difference if it happens to be a matter of business.'

'I suppose so.'

'You've seen something of the world; now here's your opportunity to look at a slice more. And, as you know the language, it seems to me you're just the man. You can talk to the Russians straight from the shoulder.'

He got up from his chair and went to look out of the window, his broad, slightly stooping back turned to his nephew. The sunlight seemed to touch his body with a fringe of fire.

'These Russians now. We've had a lot of dealings with them. Always found them keen men of business — straightforward. Don't know what they're like in other ways, of course. Politics, all that nonsense — nothing to do with us. This is a timber firm, out to buy material in the best market. If the Russians have the right stuff at the right price, why shouldn't we take it, eh?'

He had turned to face his nephew, the cigar planted firmly in his mouth, his keen eyes peering along the line of it. It was as though he had sensed some criticism of his trading methods and had swung into the attack.

'No reason at all,' Brett said. 'What do you want me to do out there?'

'In Archangel? Oh, nothing much, really. The business is working smoothly enough. It'll be more a diplomatic visit than anything else. Friendly exchanges and all that. I hope you can drink vodka.'

'In moderation.'

'Ha! From all I hear, these Russians don't know what moderation is. They'll drink you under the table if you aren't careful. But I dare say you've got a hard head; all the Mannings have; always have had. Not like those damned Bretts, eh? And when you

15

come back, if everything is satisfactory, we shall have to see about a partnership for you. No, don't thank me. For one thing, it was always looked upon as a matter of course; and for another, you haven't got it yet.'

He slumped down in his chair again and drew some of the papers towards him. Having slipped a pair of horn-rimmed glasses on his nose he reached for a pen.

'You can go along and have a look at the ship now if you like. *Silver Tassie*; there's a queer name for a steamer. Scottish, I suppose.'

Brett, seeing that his uncle was beginning to write and taking his last speech for a dismissal, moved towards the door. As he opened it Robertson looked up.

'Oh, I forgot. There's a — ah — message for you.' He hunted about among the untidy piles of papers on the desk and found a slip on which some words were scribbled. 'It's from Jennie Walsh. She rang up.' He peered over the tops of his spectacles at his nephew. 'She wants you to go up to their house this evening.'

Robertson coughed. There was an air of disapproval about him. 'You'll go?'

'Oh, yes,' Brett answered. 'I'll be pleased to.'

'Humph!' The disapproval was very

marked. Mrs Walsh, Jennifer's mother, had been related by marriage to Mrs George Manning, though there had been no blood relationship. But she also was artistic, and Robertson feared that too much contact with such people might taint Brett, Manning though he was.

Brett noticed his uncle's displeasure and knew very well what was the cause of it. He laughed. 'You needn't worry. I shan't catch anything harmful. I was inoculated against Artists' Disease in the Army.'

Robertson frowned for a moment; then he laughed too. It was a harsh, grating laugh, like that of a man unused to such indulgence.

'Get along with you. You wouldn't have caught it anyway; damned if you would. You're a Manning; you're a Manning all through. Artists' Disease, indeed!'

He ceased laughing and his face settled back into its normal severe lines. 'All right, then; go and take a look at the ship. You may find an old friend of yours on board.'

'An old friend? Who's that?'

'Never mind who. Go and have a look.'

Brett closed the door behind him and went in search of the *Silver Tassie*. He found that the ship had not long started discharging cargo; the well-decks fore and aft were still packed high with timber, held in place by upright spars. He paused at a little distance from the steamer, examining her with the experienced eye of one brought up within sight and sound of shipping.

The *Silver Tassie* was not a very modern ship. It was many years since she had glided down the slipway into the busy Clyde; but she was freshly painted and had altogether a well-built and well-cared-for appearance. She was not a slattern, as some old ships are, streaked with rust and grimy with soot; she had aged gracefully, like a prim, self-respecting lady. She was about 2,000 tons gross, a three-islander, with a counter stern and straight bows. Her funnel was rather tall and thin, painted a pale blue with three silver bands near the top; and her masts stood up very straight and sober, without any rakishness to give an impression of speed that she did not possess.

There did not appear to be a great deal of accommodation. Cargo was obviously the primary consideration and passengers of secondary importance. No doubt a few could be squeezed in amidships, but Brett guessed there was not likely to be anything very luxurious about his voyage to Russia. Not that he minded: he had become used to austere living in the Army; and when you travelled in a ship such as this you did not expect the kind of stateroom allotted to first-class passengers in the *Queen Mary* — you fitted yourself in between the cargo and made the best of things as they were.

Although the wind was cold, the *Silver Tassie* had a warm look about her as the sun glinted on masts and upper-works, throwing long shadows on to the quay and imprinting there a grotesquely distorted image of the vessel. Electric cranes, looking like overgrown giraffes, were engaged in lifting slings of timber from the decks. With surprisingly graceful movements they swung their loads in an arc over the quayside and lowered them smoothly to the busy little fork-lift trucks that darted to and fro between ship and shed. There was no pause; the work went on steadily; the burden on the *Silver Tassie* shrank by imperceptible degrees; and by imperceptible degrees the Plimsoll mark upon her side rose higher and higher above the level of the water.

Brett, his initial inspection completed, walked across to the ship, and for a moment forgot to exercise that care which is necessary when walking along a busy wharf; he forgot to keep his gaze lifted to the cranes. He heard a sudden yell of warning: 'Look out there!' Then he was falling forward on to hands and knees, propelled by a violent thrust in the back.

A moment later he was hauled to his feet again and heard a thick, hoarse voice in his ear. 'Trying to get your ruddy head knocked off? Is that it?' Then the expression of the voice changed to one of surprise and delight, and Brett felt another thump on the shoulder. 'Well, if it isn't you, me old sparring partner! Now who'd have thought you'd have bin walking about with your eyes shut when a ship was unloading? Lucky I was by to knock you out of harm's way.'

Brett rubbed his knees. 'Lucky you were, Grill. But did you have to make it quite so painful? What are you doing here anyway? I thought you'd left the firm.'

'So I have, boy; so I have. I'm a sailor again. A life on the ocean wave, a life on the rolling deep! How long it'll last, I couldn't say. Till I'm fed up with it, I s' pose.'

'You're looking well on it.'

'Don't get no thinner, eh? Well, why should I?'

'Why, indeed?'

Grill Butler was about six feet tall and as thick as a beer-barrel. He had little that could properly be called a neck, for his head, which was round and hard and hairless as a cannon-ball, seemed to grow almost directly

20

from his shoulders. On either side of it were two crumpled cauliflower ears and in the middle of his face, as if to complete a triangle of unsightly protuberances, was a nose like a piece of putty that a child has been playing with. This nose had, in fact, been so kneaded and pummelled and battered that it appeared to have spread over nearly twice the area of face that nature had originally allotted to it. The result was that the nostrils had in the course of time become almost completely closed to the passage of air, and when Grill breathed it was with a noise like that of bellows operating on a sulky fire. His face was fleshy, and from it his eyes peered out like two glass alleys of rather inferior quality, that had been stuck in an undercooked boiled pudding.

His arms were of almost freakish length and his hands so large that he could have gripped a football in either of them with no more difficulty than a boy would experience in picking up a marble. His stomach bulged over the waist-band of his trousers like the sail of a square-rigged ship with a following wind, and it was supported by a leather belt, three inches wide and nearly half an inch thick, secured by a solid brass buckle at a point directly beneath his navel. When he laughed the laugh seemed to have its birth in these lower regions, for the whole mass of bulging flesh heaved and quivered as though an earthquake were troubling it. In fact, the sight of Grill Butler laughing was worth travelling a mile to see, for his eyes closed, his mouth gaped wide open to exhibit a range of gold-filled teeth, and his entire body from head to foot shook like a monstrous jelly.

But the borderline between his laughter and his rage was narrow: you could laugh with Grill Butler, but it was unwise to laugh at him. The grotesque formation of his body made him an easy butt for coarse humour, yet that very grotesqueness made him all the more sensitive to mockery; and when with extreme sensitiveness are allied a strong arm and a heavy fist it is well to beware of mockery.

Grill stabbed a thumb over his shoulder to indicate the *Silver Tassie*.

'I'm one of her crew now. Able-bodied Seaman James Butler, that's me.'

'Oh, then you'll be the old friend my uncle was referring to. He said I'd find one on board. What made you go back to the sea?'

Butler stuck his thumbs in the waist-band of his trousers, taking the weight of those monstrous hands off his arms. He was wearing a blue jersey and a leather wind-cheater, and hanging from the belt at the back was a pig-skin sheath, containing a long seaman's knife with a carved wooden handle. A stubble of short hairs gave the lower part of his face a slightly blackened appearance, as though some one had been rubbing it with coal-dust.

'What made me go back? Wanted a change. I always was the one for chopping and changing, as you well know. Can't stay fixed for long, not me.'

'I expect you've got itchy feet.'

'Maybe. I reckon it's the gipsy in me.' He laughed, but it was only a minor eruption; there was no more than a slight quivering of the stomach. Anything more unlike a gipsy in appearance than Grill Butler would have been difficult to imagine; but he had certainly been one for changing jobs ever since, as a boy, he had joined the Navy to see the world. Brett had often heard the story of this early life. 'Didn't know no better, see? I was just a nipper, hardly dry behind the lugs, if you know what I mean.'

But even at that age he must have been a singularly unattractive youth, for within a month he had earned the nickname, Gorilla, which was later to be shortened to Grill and stick to him for the rest of his life.

In the Navy Grill Butler acquired two attributes of questionable value — a tattooed chest and the ability to box. The tattoo consisted of a representation of the Eiffel Tower, its base at the level of his waist and its pinnacle symmetrically placed between his nipples. On one side of the Tower were the words 'I love' and on the other side was the name 'Gladys'. But the Gladys affair had been short-lived; a pork butcher of ample means had taken the girl and left the sailor, if not exactly heart-broken, certainly much provoked. In white-hot indignation he had gone back to the tattooist and ordered him to write the word 'Cancelled' like a date stamp diagonally across the 'I love' while 'Gladys' was almost obliterated by the single word 'Bitch'.

With these records of youthful error imprinted on his chest, if not his heart, and the Eiffel Tower bravely standing between, he applied himself with an increased vigour to his other love — the ring. There his success was greater; so much greater, in fact, that an astute manager, seeing in the young naval champion a means of lining his own pocket, advanced the money to buy Grill out of the Service and proceeded to push him rapidly up the ladder of professional boxing.

Grill might well have reached the top if he had stuck at it. He had the physique and he was no mean performer — of the happy, battering type, quite content to take blow for blow and not worry too much about defence. But he tired of the ring. 'It was,' he would say, 'no occupation for a gentleman.' No one could understand why this should have barred him from it, but it was suspected that the true reason for his retirement was that he could no longer endure the cries of 'Come on, Gladys!' and 'Up the Eiffel Tower!' that greeted him whenever he appeared. He drew the crowds, for, win or lose, there were always fireworks when Grill Butler was engaged in a fight; and he made good money, but he could not put up with the chaff. If a man laughed at him he was inclined to take that man apart and see what he was made of; but when a few thousand people are laughing at you, you cannot easily take them all apart, however strong you may be. So Grill quarrelled with his manager and took a job in a circus, under the stage name of Hercules the Second.

But he tired of that too. 'It was a damn silly life, see? Lifting weights an' putting 'em down again. Where's the sense in it? It don't get you anywhere.' After that he became in turn lorry driver, farm hand, night watchman, brush salesman, pneumatic drill operator, artists' model, and bricklayer's labourer. When war broke out he rejoined the Navy and did five years' service on the convoy routes of the

Atlantic, the Mediterranean, and the Arctic. 'It was the longest job I ever had. No way of getting out of it, you see; except by being blown to bits, and I didn't fancy none of that lark.' He came out of the Navy with a DSM and a nasty scar across the upper reaches of the Eiffel Tower caused by a flying shell splinter. For this devilish piece of work he never forgave the Germans. 'Vandalism — that's what it was — sheer bloody vandalism. Wouldn't have minded if they'd just sliced off that bitch, Gladys; but they never oughter've touched my Eiffel Tower — never.'

It was after the war that he drifted into Manning's timber wharf. He was now thirty-nine but still not settled. Brett, just growing out of adolescence to manhood, took an instant liking to the battered ex-pugilist; the ugliness of the man was even an added attraction; it fascinated him. It was he who suggested that Grill should teach him to box, an invitation that was accepted with delight. Grill had put on weight since his early days in the ring, his stomach had expanded, but he was still tough and remarkably agile for one so heavily built. And the stomach was not all fat; there was muscle there too, as Brett was soon to discover.

'Hit me in the guts, then; go on, boy, hit

me; hit me as hard as you can. Don't be scared of killing me.'

Brett, thus invited, had lashed out at the great belly, half expecting his fist to sink in up to the wrist. But the belly had suddenly become tough, like gutta-percha, and his fist had rebounded, painfully jarred. Grill had erupted into volcanic laughter.

'Did you feel it, boy? Hard, ain't it? Muscle control — that's the secret. I'll teach you, boy; I'll teach you.'

Robertson Manning had not disapproved of this friendship between his nephew and the gross, cannon-ball-headed ex-pug. It would harden the boy, make a man of him. 'So that villain, Butler, is teaching you the noble art of self-defence, eh? Well, well; learn what you can. It can't do you any harm and it may come in useful one day.'

Grill had Brett lifting baulks of timber to toughen his muscles. They fixed up a punch-bag in one of the sheds, and Grill showed the way a straight left should be thrust out to jolt an opponent. 'Not that I ever had much use for a straight left meself. Maybe I'd be prettier now if I had.' He exploded with laughter. He could joke about his own appearance, but, like Cyrano de Bergerac, he was quick to answer with a blow the same jest on the lips of anyone else. Brett,

aware of this sensitiveness on the part of his
sparring partner, was careful always to avoid
any reference to his singular personal
appearance. Thus a strong bond of friendship
was forged between the strangely assorted
pair, and it was this more than anything else
that kept Grill so long with the firm of Josiah
Manning, Son, and Company. But when
Brett was called up to do his National Service
Grill felt the tie no longer, and within a week
he was off again on his ramblings. From that
day to this Brett had not seen him.

'I'm glad you're with the *Silver Tassie*,'
Brett said. 'You'll be company for me.'

Grill's forehead wrinkled. 'How you mean
— company?'

'I'm sailing with you to Archangel.'

'You are? Why, that's fine, just fine. What
are you going there for?'

'Business.'

Grill nodded solemnly. When he spoke
again his voice held a note of respect. 'Oh, ay;
you've grown up now. You're a man of
importance. Reckon I'll be hardly good
enough for the likes of you.'

Brett slapped him on the shoulder. 'Don't
be a fool, Grill. What do you take me for?
You're my pal, just the same as always. How
about a few rounds with the gloves, eh? What
do you say to that — sparring partner?'

Grill's eyes sparkled. 'When? This evening?'

'No, not this evening. I have an appointment. Tomorrow, if that's all right for you.'

'Okay, boy. It'll be like old times. Remember that straight left.' He fingered the bicep muscle in Brett's arm. 'They haven't let you get soft in the Army, have they? No; that feels all right. Tomorrow then — and watch your step.'

Brett had tea with his aunt and his three cousins. Robertson Manning had certainly not committed the same folly as his brother, George, for Mrs Robertson came from a solid commercial family, and her own virtues were also of a solid, utilitarian variety. She had no pretensions to beauty, and this lack of physical attraction, which may perhaps even have commended her to the forthright Robertson, had been handed down to her three daughters. They were, in fact, all very much alike and all peculiarly equine in feature, having long, narrow faces and prominent teeth.

Brett was rather sorry for the girls: it seemed so very unlikely that any one of them would ever rouse feelings of desire in the heart of a young man. Robertson himself was barely civil to his daughters; he had never forgiven them for those three successive disappointments of being told that Mrs

Manning had failed in her duty of providing him with a son. It was Brett who had come to fill this gap, and it was on him that Robertson lavished whatever affection there might be in his tough old heart. This obvious preference for Brett might have been calculated to kindle feelings of jealousy in the daughters, but it did not. Though physically unattractive they were singularly good-natured girls, and looked upon their cousin with a sisterly admiration that was quite unmixed with any resentment.

If only, Brett thought, they had been like Jennifer Walsh, there would have been any number of young suitors eager for their favours. But of course few girls were like Jennifer. Indeed, he fully believed there was not another in the world as attractive as she.

'I'm going round to the Walshes' this evening,' Brett said. 'Don't wait up for me if I'm late.'

But he knew that, however late he might be, one of them would be sure to be sitting up for him. Not his aunt; she invariably went to bed at ten; but Jane or Lavinia or Freda, or even all three, would be there when he came in, ready to make him a hot drink and fetch biscuits. They would always protest that they had not stayed up purposely and that they were not in the least tired, really they weren't;

but Brett was not misled. He wished they would not do it; but he believed they derived some peculiar satisfaction from doing these little things for him.

There was quite a party at the Walshes'. Frank Walsh was an architect, a tall, thin, stooping man who bent towards anyone to whom he was talking, like a reed breathed upon by the wind. His wife had been an actress before he married her, and it was only necessary to look at Jennifer to see just what she had been like at the time of her stage career.

'I must banish the child,' Mrs Walsh would say, fluttering her hand in one of those theatrical gestures that she still retained. 'She reminds me too poignantly of my vanished youth.'

Not that she could be said to have lost her own beauty, in spite of a tendency to plumpness. It was indeed an attractive active plumpness, and altogether she was a vivid, dark, attractive woman, totally unlike her languid, equable husband.

'I hear you're going to Russia, Brett,' Frank Walsh remarked. 'Mind you don't get into trouble with the secret police.'

'How on earth did you know about it?' Brett asked. 'I knew nothing myself until this afternoon.'

'These things have a way of getting about. Going on a diplomatic mission?'

'The fact is, I really haven't the least idea yet why I am going. Uncle Bobs seems to think it might be good for trade relations. The personal touch and all that.'

'You must be careful they don't try to brain-wash you.'

'Don't be silly, Daddy,' said Jennifer, suddenly appearing from behind them. 'What could anyone hope to wash out of Brett's brain?'

'You might be surprised,' Brett said. 'I am a very clever man. Have you forgotten that I was in Army Intelligence? Only the best brains get in that, my girl.'

Frank Walsh drifted away and became engaged in conversation with a young and highly unsuccessful composer of the ultra-modern school.

'I wish I were coming with you,' Jennifer said to Brett. 'I'm sure it will be exciting.'

'I don't know about excitement, but I certainly wish you were coming, too.' He took the girl's arm and drew her away from the crowd. 'You're looking very pretty tonight, Jennie.'

'Only tonight?'

'Tonight and always.'

It had taken Brett a long while to realize

that he was in love with Jennifer. They had always been good friends; from earliest childhood they had played together. Perhaps that had been the reason; perhaps he had taken her rather too much for granted. Only when his military service had called him away had it been borne in upon him how integral a part of his life she had become and how deep a gap would be left in that life if he were never to see her again. During his time in Germany this girl, with her dark hair and smiling eyes, had been much in his thoughts; he had looked eagerly for her letters, and in reading them he had seemed to hear her voice and her happy laughter. He had known then that no one else could fill her place, that when he returned he would ask her to be his wife.

He said: 'When I come back from Russia Uncle Bobs has as good as promised me a partnership.'

Jennifer put a hand on his arm in an eager gesture of congratulation. 'That will be lovely for you, Brett. I am so glad.'

'Are you — really? It might make a lot of difference to me — to us.'

'In what way?'

Brett looked round the crowded room, hazy with tobacco smoke. Everyone seemed to be talking animatedly. He turned again to Jennifer.

'Come for a walk,' he said. 'It's a fine night and nobody will miss us. Perhaps I'll tell you.'

★ ★ ★

It was late when Brett walked home. He felt that the evening had been entirely successful, that he had attained what he had most desired. His uncle might not approve of the engagement, but he was bound to come round in the end. Even a man as craggy as Robertson would not be able to resist Jennifer's charm; he would just have to come round.

Brett felt that he had everything to look forward to on his return from Russia — marriage to Jennifer, and a partnership in the firm. Who could ask for more?

He looked up and saw a star, brilliantly red, flare across the northern sky. A red star — the star of Russia — flaming across his path! A more superstitious man might have seen in this an omen, a warning not to look too far ahead, not to count upon the future.

Brett saw the star but ignored the omen. In his mind the Russian journey was already accomplished.

2

Dark Encounter

'Not so much excitement in these waters as there used to be a few years back,' remarked Captain Brownrigg. 'What with E-boats, U-boats, planes, and mines, there was never a dull moment. You won't remember much of that, I suppose.'

'I was at school then,' Brett said. He looked down towards the bows of the ship, watching them cleave through the grey waters of the North Sea, and tried to imagine what this journey had been like in war-time. No doubt Brownrigg could tell him. He had been through it all.

The master of the *Silver Tassie* was a thick-set, middle-aged man with greying hair and a round, brick-red face. He had invited Brett to come up to the bridge as soon as the pilot had been dropped. Brett accepted the invitation readily, knowing that he was privileged. Though the ship had accommodation for four passengers, Brett was the only one on this particular voyage, and possibly Captain Brownrigg was glad of someone to talk to besides the other ship's officers.

The *Silver Tassie* was carrying a cargo of electrical machinery and motor vehicles. The vehicles were for Iceland and the machinery, stowed in the lower sections of the holds, was for delivery to Russia.

'Means a longer voyage, having to go to Reykjavik,' Brownrigg explained. 'We could have kept pretty near the Norwegian coast otherwise. This will be more like the Arctic convoy route we used to follow during the War. We kept as far away from Norway then as we could manage.'

'You were on that run, then?'

'Once or twice. That was plenty.'

The motion of the ship became more uneasy as she met the North Sea rollers. Brett was fascinated by the lift and fall of the bows; it seemed scarcely believable that this stout vessel, so stable, so nearly motionless in harbour, should now be lifted and shaken as though there were no more weight in her than in a toy ship that a child carries under its arm. He glanced at Captain Brownrigg; the man's face was expressionless; probably he took every manifestation of the power of Nature in a perfectly matter of fact way, never pausing to think deeply of causes, but only of effects, which altered the behaviour of his ship and made it necessary for him to take this or that particular course of action.

'Ever been to Russia before?' Brownrigg asked suddenly.

'No,' Brett said.

'You've had a lot to do with them perhaps?'

'Very little really. I know the language.'

'They're a strange people. Dashed if I can ever understand them properly. Somehow, there's no getting inside their minds. You can't see how they work.'

He gave a little tug at the peak of his cap, pulling it down more firmly on his head as the wind freshened from the north-east. Brett began to experience a slight feeling of queasiness in the stomach, and wondered whether he was going to be seasick. He hoped he would not make a fool of himself in that way. He would have liked to leave the bridge and go to his cabin and lie down, but Brownrigg was speaking again.

'Take the War now. They never seemed to have a notion what it meant to bring convoys through the Barents Sea — not a notion. Or maybe they were just plain callous; I don't know. Certainly they didn't help us much from their end; just seemed to delight in being obstructive. I'll give you an example. There was a crowd of us Merchant Navy fellows ashore in a Russian hospital — wounded, you see — frost-bitten and God knows what else. This was in 1942, and our people sent out a medical unit to help look after us. But the Russians wouldn't even let them land. Can you beat it? We were their allies; we'd been bringing them war material, hadn't we? But no; the unit had to go back in the next convoy home. You'd hardly believe it.

'And all the time they were yelling out for more deliveries, more guns, more tanks, more ammunition. In my opinion we could have made better use of the stuff ourselves. Half of it went to the bottom, anyway. There was no gratitude; well, perhaps you couldn't expect that; but a little more co-operation would have been welcome.

'Not that they treated us badly — not personally. It always seems to me that as individuals they're all right, the majority of them; nobody could be more friendly; but behind the individual is this great impersonal monster, the Communist State, and with that you're up against something that's blind and ruthless, and, so it seems to me, frightened.'

'Do you get much trouble in Russian ports nowadays?'

'Very little. Things go pretty smoothly as long as you stick to the rules. Of course, now and then some damn fool of a deck hand goes ashore, drinks too much vodka, and tries to pull the town apart. Then he lands in gaol and there's a bit of a to-do; but that could happen anywhere. You've got to abide by the laws of the country, and Russians don't take any more kindly to having their places smashed up than anybody else. Can't blame them for that.'

As the ship steamed farther and farther out to sea and the land slid away in haze on the port quarter, the wind grew stronger and colder. Spray came flying over the bows and the fore-deck, and the tarpaulins stretched over the hatches gleamed with moisture. The ship began to roll heavily, and Brett felt ill. The hot, bitter taste of seasickness rose in his throat; he swallowed; it rose again. His head felt leaden and his eyes burned.

Captain Brownrigg stared at him. 'My God! you're looking green. You'd better go below and lie down for a while.'

'I think I had,' Brett said.

Lying on his bunk in the small cabin that had been allotted to him, Brett felt a little better. In the horizontal position one seemed to be less susceptible to the effect of the ship's rolling. He tried to think of more pleasant things than seasickness, and the pleasantest subject he could think of was the girl whose photograph was pinned to the bulkhead opposite the bunk. Jennifer Walsh was to become his wife when he returned from Russia: he concentrated his mind on that thought. Married to Jennifer and a partner in the firm: there was something to look forward to; that, if anything, ought to act as an antidote to sickness.

But, thinking of the bright future that lay ahead, he experienced a sudden superstitious qualm, a feeling that to count upon anything so desirable was to tempt Fate to take it from him. Who could tell what might happen before this ship again reached home? There were such hazards as storms and rocks and sandbanks; such disasters as wrecks. He touched the wood of his bunk and laughed at himself for doing so.

The ship lurched violently, like a drunken man. The cabin seemed to gyrate before Brett's eyes; it would not be still. He became nauseatingly aware of the smell of fresh paint, and he felt that never before had he realized quite how horrible a smell it was. He wondered gloomily whether he would ever again be able to face the sight of food. He began to search the cabin for a bucket.

Two days later the *Silver Tassie* was passing between the Orkneys and the Shetlands, and Brett had recovered from his sickness and was regaining an interest in the voyage.

'You're looking better,' Captain Brownrigg

remarked. 'A shade thinner perhaps; but you'll soon make up for lost time. They always do. Never knew a man yet who didn't eat his head off once he was over his bout.'

Brett grinned a little sheepishly. 'I suppose you've never been seasick?'

'Me? Lord, yes. Not for a good many years, though. But I know what it's like. It's something you don't forget. Personally, I can't stand a man who goes about boasting that he's never been sick, as if it was something to be proud of. If a man's been endowed with a cast-iron stomach it's Nature that should take the credit, not him. You'll be all right now, though; you've had your whack.'

'I hope so,' Brett said. 'Once is enough. I thought my inside was coming up.'

'You should have taken more grub. Seasickness is always worse on an empty stomach; it's got nothing to work on, see? By the way, I believe you know one of our seamen, a feller named Butler.'

'Grill Butler? Yes, I know him. He taught me to box.'

'Hm! Did he? Well, if you could teach him to control his temper it might save him a deal of trouble.'

'Why? What's he been up to?'

'Oh, nothing much,' Brownrigg said grimly.

'Half killed one of his shipmates, that's all. Looks as though he may be on a serious charge when we get back home. You can't do that sort of thing; you just can't do it. Damned nuisance, too.'

Brett was perturbed. He had scarcely seen Grill since sailing day; he had spent most of the time lying on his bunk and waiting for the sickness to pass. He was sorry to hear that Grill had been in trouble.

'Do you know what it was about? Butler wouldn't beat anybody up without some cause.'

'I don't know.' Brownrigg spoke impatiently. It was obvious that the affair had angered him, upsetting the harmony of his ship. 'Maybe the feller insulted him, called him names. I don't know. You might be able to get a bit of sense out of Butler, seeing he's a friend of yours. I've spoken to him, but he's just sullen. Seems to think that everybody is down on him.'

'Perhaps he'll talk to me.'

'Perhaps he will. I can't get much out of him.'

Grill talked to Brett readily enough. He was feeling injured; he felt that everyone had condemned him out of hand, refusing to see that he had right on his side. But Brett was a friend. Brett would listen to him and understand.

'It was like this: there was four of us in the fo'c'sle playing cards, see? Me and this bastard, Lock, and a couple of others — pals of his. You've seen Lock? No? He's a long-haired know-all, a proper Teddy-boy when he's ashore — drape jacket, string tie, drainpipe pants, creep shoes, and all the rest. Gets a permanent wave in his blasted hair, too. You know the type. Oughter be swep' up off the streets and took away in a dust-cart.'

Grill's mouth twisted up in disgust. 'Him and me, we didn't see eye to eye in the matter of a card under the table. I said to him, 'Sonny,' I said, 'you play straight in this school or you get to hell out of it.' I was quite civil, see?

'He looks at me with a sneer on his kisser. 'Who says so?' he asks. 'I do,' I says. 'A lot I care what you say, you ugly old bastard,' he says. 'You wanter get your face lifted. You wanter get a crane to work on it'.'

Grill reddened at the memory. He was standing with his back leaning against the starboard bulwark on the afterdeck, his elbows resting upon it.

'Insults, you see. Not content with cheating, he has to fling insults in me face as well. 'Why,' I says, 'you little jumped-up runt; who do you think you're talking to?'

''I'm talking to you,' he says, 'and if you

43

don't like it you can do the other thing'.'

Grill took hold of Brett's arm, and Brett could feel the thick fingers biting into his flesh.

'Now, I ask you,' Grill said. 'Would anybody what calls hisself a man take that without any protest?'

'What did you do?' Brett asked.

Grill released Brett's arm and spat over the side of the ship. The wind caught his spittle and carried it away into the sea.

'Do? I'll tell you what I did. I was calm, I tell you; very calm. I said to him, 'Sonny, you may think you're mighty clever, but you ain't so clever as you think you are. Either you take back them words and beg my pardon or you get your pretty face stove in.' That was fair enough; that was telling him straight, wasn't it?'

'What did he say to that?'

'He said, 'I ain't taking nothing back. I'll tell you again you're an ugly-faced old bastard. You oughter wear a mask, so's not to make people sick.'

'God Almighty! There's limits to what a man can take and still keep his self-respeck. I had a fistful of cards and I flung 'em in his kisser. 'You've asked for it,' I says. 'Now you're going to get it.'

'Then what you think he done?' Grill's

44

voice was hoarse with incredulity, as though he could still scarcely bring himself to believe that it had really happened. 'He pulled a razor on me — a razor! I ask you; what sort of a weapon is that for a seaman?

'He sliced me with it once.' Grill pulled up his sleeve and showed a strip of adhesive bandage on his left arm. 'By God, I'd have rammed it down his filthy throat if the others hadn't pulled me off. But he won't try that lark again in a hurry — not with me, he won't.'

'Did you damage him much?' Brett asked.

'Not as much as I'd have liked to. Maybe he ain't so pretty as he was; but he'll be all right.'

'You know it may be a matter for the police when we get home?'

'When we get home! Ah, but when will that be? I never worry meself about what may happen at the end of the voyage. Sufficient for the day, boy; sufficient for the day.'

He seemed to have recovered all his good humour, having got the story off his chest. Suddenly he began to chuckle, and the chuckle grew into a laugh. Soon his whole body was shaking and quivering with laughter and his eyes were pinpoints in the gross, swollen flesh of his face. He gripped the bulwark to support him in his laughter and his voice came choking out of his body.

'You oughter have seen his face. Oh my! you oughter have seen it. Teddy-boy! Scum! But you should have seen his face.'

★　★　★

The *Silver Tassie* unloaded her motor vehicles in Reykjavik and sailed for Russia, heading eastward for North Cape and the iron-bound Kola Peninsula. The wind came cold off the sea, and at night the Aurora Borealis flung its garish streamers across the northern sky. A gale came up out of the west and blew the sea into hills around the ship; and so for two days they fought the gale and the sea, and struggled eastward, groaning and labouring.

Brett rather enjoyed the storm; it was a new experience, a new excitement. He was gratified, too, to find that there was no recurrence of seasickness; the first bout appeared to have inoculated him. So he would stand on deck, balancing himself against the roll of the ship, and watch the spindrift flying from the tops of the waves like wood-smoke blowing from a cottage chimney.

'You get it rough sometimes up here,' Captain Brownrigg explained. 'Usually later in the year than this, though. The sea isn't really deep, you understand, not like the Atlantic. But because it's comparatively shallow a wind will always whip up these big short seas that set your ship rolling. You're not feeling sick?'

Brett grinned. 'Not any more. One dose worked the oracle.'

'Glad to hear it. Some people never get over it, you know. As soon as the ship begins to roll at all, back it comes. A sailor's life simply isn't the thing for them, and that's all there is to it.'

After two days the gale died away to a whisper and the seas went down. The *Silver Tassie* increased her speed and steamed on bravely eastward.

To Brett there was added excitement in the realization that they were now within the Arctic Circle, though Captain Brownrigg, to whom he mentioned the fact, seemed completely unmoved.

'I felt that way myself when I was younger. The very names of the seas fascinated me; they seemed to have music in them — the Persian Gulf, the Bay of Bengal, the China Sea, the Sea of Okhotsk, the Gulf of Mexico. But you get over it, more's the pity. Now there's only one sea that I like, and that's a calm one.'

'Well, this one is calm enough now.'

They were standing on the starboard wing of the bridge, and all around them lay the grey, flat surface of the water, with the grey sky, like a leaden dome, closing down upon it. At the horizon where the two joined company it was scarcely possible to detect the line of demarcation; the sea and the sky were one, indistinguishable.

'Calm enough,' admitted Brownrigg. 'But I don't altogether like it. If we don't get a real thick fog off it before long, then I'm much mistaken. There's a feel of fog.'

The captain was not mistaken. By nightfall fog had closed in upon the ship like a clammy blanket, and as they groped blindly forward at slow speed the blaring siren shouted its intermittent warning into the night.

'Fog,' said Grill Butler, 'is something I do not like — not at any price. It's worse than storms. Ships in fog is like a lot of cars being driven by people with their eyes shut, relying on the horn to keep them out of trouble.'

He was keeping a look-out in the bows of the ship, and Brett, unable to sleep for the hooting of the siren, had come out to keep him company for a while. Standing there on the forecastle, it was impossible to see even the faintest outline of the bridge. It was as though the two of them were standing on a tiny island completely cut off from the rest of the world. Below they could hear the sinister gurgle of invisible water as it flowed past the slow-moving ship. The fog seemed to penetrate their clothing with damp, icy fingers; it settled in drops upon their eyelashes, and their eyes ached with the cold and the strain of trying to pierce this screen of floating moisture. Everywhere the metal of the ship dripped, wet and chilly to the touch; the deck was slippery underfoot, and at their backs was the dark, scarcely visible shape of the steam windlass.

'I was in a ship once,' Grill said, 'what ran into a proper Newfoundland Banker — thick as this here, it was, with the siren going just like ours is now. Then we heard an answering hoot, and when we hooted again the answer came again. Well, fog's no place for a couple of ships to be shaking hands in, so our captain gave the order to alter course, and gradually the other siren got fainter until at last it faded out altogether. Well, that was all right, you may say, but the funny thing was that we found out later there hadn't been any other ship in that area at that particular time — not one. What there had been though was a monster great iceberg as big as a hill, and it must have been the echo of our own siren coming back off the ice that we'd heard. Just as well too; we might have run slap-bang into it, else.'

He began to clap his hands together rhythmically, producing a noise like that of someone beating a carpet.

'Trouble with fog is you can't never tell for certain about directions. You may think a sound is coming from one point and somebody else will swear it's coming from another. There's no way of being sure; it's all trial and error, and just too bad for you if it turns out to be error.'

The siren blared out again, a long, throbbing blast. It came every two minutes; it was expected; yet each time it was a shock to the nerves, vibrating them as a certain note will vibrate a tautened wire.

'There it goes again,' said Grill hoarsely. 'Like an old cow what's lost its calf.'

He peered ahead into the fog; then suddenly he gripped Brett's arm.

'There! Did you hear that, or am I dreaming?'

Brett listened. There was nothing but the chuckle of the water; no breath of wind to sigh in the rigging and tear the fog to ribbons; no crash of wave or patter of rain.

'I don't hear anything, Grill.'

'No; it's gone now. But I thought I heard something, just for an instant. Maybe it was imagination. You get to imagining things in this damned cotton-wool. Ghosts! I reckon ghosts would be all you could see in a night like this. Proper place for ghosts too; there's plenty men what met a sudden death in these regions.'

He stamped his feet. 'Talk about cold as charity! Why don't you go below? No need for you to stay out.'

'I'll wait a bit longer,' Brett said.

'Please yourself, but I'd get me head down if I was you. There's a funny thing — when a man's a passenger in a ship he'll come out on deck as often as you please and walk about and enjoy hisself. But just you make him into a seaman and pay him for being on deck, and all he'll think about is getting below. I reckon that must be human nature — you pay for something and you value it — somebody pays you to have it and all you want is to chuck it away.'

Grill sucked his teeth loudly after delivering this brief lecture on psychology and began to hum a tune, beating time with his hands.

Again the siren of the *Silver Tassie* sent out its waves of sound, probing into the night, giving warning of the ship's presence. And as the sound died mournfully away Grill seized Brett's arm again.

'There! Now do you hear it?'

Brett answered quickly: 'Yes. Yes, I hear it now.' Faintly, like an echo from far away, came the hoot of another siren.

'I'll give them the tip on the bridge,' Grill said. 'They may be asleep.'

He moved away, and Brett could hear him turning the handle of the telephone. Then he was speaking hoarsely into the instrument. A minute later he was back.

'They heard it all right. Wanted to know if I could give them the direction. They thought it was on the port beam, but I don't think they was feeling at all sure. I said it sounded to me like dead ahead. What do you think?'

'I thought so too.'

But when it came again it seemed to Brett to be on the port bow. Yet, though it was louder, it was hard to tell; the fog seemed to muffle and spread it, so that the sound might have been all around them, like a voice echoing in an empty room.

'Blast this fog! Damn and blast the filthy muck!' Grill muttered. The siren of the *Silver Tassie* swallowed up his words in another wave of warning sound. But this time there was no answering cry. Brett wondered whether the other ship had sounded its warning simultaneously, rendering each inaudible to the other. It was a game of blind man's buff with two blind men, each trying to avoid the other and not knowing how to do so.

'Who's on the bridge?' he asked.

'Oh, the Old Man,' Grill answered. 'You wouldn't find Johnnie Brownrigg in his cabin on a night like this. He'll stick it out. The third's there with him; but if you had a whole ruddy brains-trust they couldn't tell for certain where that other ship is.'

'Pity we haven't got a radar set.'

'Ah, now that would be some use.'

Suddenly they heard again the other ship's siren, alarmingly louder and closer. It seemed to have crept up on them amazingly quickly.

'I'd swear that was on the starboard bow now,' Grill muttered. 'And there's another thing; that ship's moving a sight faster than what we are. She wouldn't have got so close in the time, else.'

He began moving restlessly, as if under some nervous compulsion. He kicked his toes against the iron bulwarks that ended in a narrow 'V' at the foremost point of the ship. He turned his head, listening first with one ear, then with the other. He made a clucking noise with his tongue. Brett had never known him to be so jumpy.

Suddenly he cried: 'Hullo, hullo! What's all this in aid of?'

The *Silver Tassie* had heeled over slightly

to port; then slowly she came up again on to an even keel.

'Altering course to starboard. What's up with their lugs on the bridge? If that don't bring us clean across that other devil's bows, then I'm a Dutchman. What's the Old Man think he's doing?'

'I'd say he was right,' Brett said. 'I thought that last hoot came from the port side. We're turning away from her.'

Grill shook his head. 'You're wrong; you're wrong. I'd stake my life you're wrong.'

They stared ahead, their ears alert for any warning. Brett felt the tension rising. He shivered, and it was not simply the cold that made him do so.

The *Silver Tassie's* siren screamed out again, and at that moment it happened. There was no avoiding the collision — nothing that anyone could do. No spin of the wheel, no reversing of the engines could have got them out of danger in time. Grill had been right, and the officers on the bridge had made a fatal error.

Simultaneously with the blare of the siren there was a crash that seemed to bludgeon the hearing like a sledgehammer driving into a man's skull. There was a noise of metal grinding, crumpling, screeching. The *Silver Tassie* shuddered, and heeled over to starboard as though a great hand had grasped her masts and pulled her on her side.

Brett was flung against the starboard bulwark with the full weight of Grill on top of him. He heard Grill cursing: 'The fools! The damned fools!'

He clawed at the bulwark, dragging himself up on to his feet, and saw the vague, amorphous mass of Grill struggling up also. He felt Grill's hand on his shoulder.

'You all right, boy? You all right?'

'Yes, yes, I'm fine.'

The *Silver Tassie* had not righted herself; the hand that had pulled her over on to her side seemed to be holding her there. The deck of the forecastle was sloping at an acute angle. The vessel shuddered again, and seemed to slip down and sideways, as though sliding down an inclined plane. She slipped a little way with a tearing, squealing noise, a noise to set the teeth on edge — halted momentarily, slipped a little farther, and halted again. Brett could hear the hissing roar of escaping steam, and, strangely dwarfed in the immensity of clamour, the voices of men shouting, as though at a great distance.

Grill dragged at his arm. His voice was hoarse and urgent. 'Come along, boy; come along. She's sinking.' He turned and led the way, groping through fog and darkness across the tilted forecastle, until they came to the ladder on the port side. They went quickly down the ladder and found that the fore-deck, even on the higher port side, was already under six inches of ice-cold water, which came swirling and tugging at their legs. As they began to wade through it the deck beneath their feet gave another staggering lunge downward with a great squeal of iron on iron, and a flood of water came up from the hidden starboard side, engulfing them to the waist.

'Hurry, boy, hurry!' Grill shouted urgently. 'She'll be gone in a minute.'

The freezing coldness of the Arctic water seized Brett like an icy band around the waist. He fought for breath, struggling forward against the flood. Once his foot struck against some obstacle hidden below the water, and he staggered forward, splashing and floundering, with the bitter taste of salt upon his lips. Then he was up again and once more moving on, until suddenly he heard Grill yell out in amazement:

'God's truth! What's this?'

He came up with Grill and found what appeared to be a dark wall of iron confronting them.

'The ship!' Grill cried. 'The other ship!'

There it was, the iron stem of the vessel that had rammed the *Silver Tassie*, thrust into her side like a great wedge. It had struck just forward of the bridge, sliced open a gap big enough for a railway engine to drive through, and had pushed the smaller vessel over on to her side with irresistible force. For a few minutes the momentum of this unknown ship had supported the *Silver Tassie*, but now, as her holds filled with water and the heavy machinery of her cargo dragged her down, she was slipping off the wedge, rending herself free, and settling lower and lower in the flood.

Brett looked up towards the top of the iron cliff that barred the way. Vaguely he thought he could discern the shapes of men moving, and hear their puny voices above the noise of escaping steam and grinding metal.

He felt lost and helpless, as though shut in a steel-walled prison with water rising all around him and no way out. For there was no way out — no way but the sea, this bitter, icy, northern sea that could kill a man with its grip as surely as the hangman's noose. And that way led only to the grave.

Again he felt a movement under his feet; and then there was nothing solid for him to stand on and the water closed over his head. He came up almost at once, striking out desperately with arms and legs. He felt a pain in his hand as it struck against something hard and ungiving. The ship! The ship that was killing him!

He looked up despairingly, and a cry for help died in his throat. Useless to cry out. There was no help for him; nothing but a brief and hopeless struggle that must end in only one way.

A surge of anger rose in him — anger that thus should be the end of all his hopes and ambitions; this senseless snuffing out of a life that had held so much promise. In his anger he struck again at the ship. This was the enemy, this that had killed him. And, in striking, his hand came upon a rope.

Instinctively he gripped it, peering through stinging eyes blinded by salt water, fog, and darkness. In front of him he could just make out the rope sides and wooden rungs of a Jacob's ladder hanging down from the bulwarks of the ship. Brett took a firmer grip on the ladder and pulled himself up until his chest was clear of the water. Then he looked round for Grill.

He shouted, almost screaming the name. 'Grill! Grill! Where are you?' It was unthinkable that he should be saved and his friend should perish.

He shouted again; and suddenly a flurry of spray was dashed into his eyes, blinding him. Then he felt something strike his leg, groping. He clung to the ladder with one hand and reached down into the water, seizing the collar of Grill's coat.

'The ladder. Grip the ladder, man.'

He heard Grill's voice, gasping. 'Okay, boy; I got it. I'm okay. You climb.'

Using his arms, Brett pulled himself clear of the water and found the bottom rung of the ladder with his feet. Then, his dripping clothes like a leaden weight upon his shoulders, he began to climb.

Looking back upon it later, it seemed hardly believable that no more than five minutes should have passed between the moment of the collision and the moment when strong hands grasped him at the top of the ladder and hauled him to safety. Five minutes only, and in that short time a ship had been killed. For as Brett stood with the water dripping from him on to this strange deck beneath his feet he glimpsed the last dim shadow of the *Silver Tassie*, like a ghostly presence in the fog, as she slid helplessly to her icy death.

There was only one sound coming faintly

out of the darkness — the voice of a man crying 'Help, help, help!' Then that, too, faded, and there remained nothing of the *Silver Tassie* but two survivors, dripping and shivering upon the deck of an alien ship.

3

The *Gregory Kotovsky*

'My name is Govorov. I understand from my chief officer that you speak Russian.'

'That is so,' Brett said.

He and Grill were sitting in a cabin that was, by the standards of British merchant ships, almost luxuriously furnished, in a heavy, ornate style. There was a thick carpet on the floor, a polished mahogany table behind which Captain Govorov was sitting, and plush-upholstered chairs. The electric lamps were fixed to the panelled walls with brackets of twisted brass decorated with a kind of filigree work, and the shades were of frosted glass patterned like the globes of Victorian oil-lamps. The whole effect was of somewhat oppressive opulence.

'It is fortunate that you do speak our language,' said Captain Govorov; 'since I fear that none of us speaks yours. The lack of a common tongue would have made communication difficult.'

Brett, in dry clothes and with a glass of vodka inside him, was feeling physically none the worse for his immersion in the ice-cold waters of the Arctic Ocean. But his mind was far from being at rest. He believed the man facing him to be little better than a murderer. He believed that on him must rest much of the blame for the loss of the *Silver Tassie*, and the death of almost all her crew.

It was possible, of course, that a boat might have got away, but it was unlikely; there had been so little time, so much confusion. It was possible, too, that even now some poor devils might be freezing to death upon a float. Yet this man, Govorov, whose almost criminal neglect of precautions had precipitated the tragedy, had not even ordered a search to be made. He had driven his ship on into the night, away from the scene of the disaster, as though it were no concern of his to search for survivors.

'You are now,' went on the Russian captain, 'on board the *Gregory Kotovsky*, ship of the USSR. I trust that during your stay with us you will be entirely comfortable.'

It was almost, Brett thought, like a landlady welcoming a guest. The incongruity struck him as grimly humorous, but he felt no inclination to smile.

Govorov had a narrow face with high cheekbones and deepset eyes of a soft, strangely liquid brown. His eyebrows were like the tufts of an artist's brush and his black hair was receding from a brow criss-crossed with the deep furrows that time, and possibly care, had ploughed. His nose was long and sharp with curling nostrils, his lips full and rather moist. He wore a moustache, and the pointedness of his chin was enhanced by a neat, tapering beard. His ears were peculiarly small, as though they had stopped growing when he was a child and had never regained proportion. There was an air of nobility about him, but a tired nobility; it was as though he were infinitely weary of life and would not have been sorry to relinquish it.

'I have no doubt,' Brett answered, 'that we shall be comfortable enough — far more comfortable than any of our shipmates who may be adrift in lifeboats or on rafts.'

As he was speaking he looked very pointedly at Govorov, and Govorov did not meet his gaze.

'In such a night it would have been useless to continue searching. We did what we could.'

'You sank our ship.'

'That was an unfortunate accident. At sea disasters occur. One cannot always avoid them. I am, I assure you, deeply sorry.'

Brett felt Grill pulling at his sleeve. 'What's he saying?' Grill asked hoarsely.

'He says he's sorry he sank our ship.'

'Bleedin' hell! Sorry! I should think so, an' all. Why didn't he look around for survivors?'

'He says it would have been hopeless.'

'He didn't try very hard. And why was he going at that speed in fog? Must have been doing fifteen knots to slice into us like that.'

Captain Govorov broke in in his deep voice. 'Your friend does not speak Russian? What does he wish to know?'

'He wants to know why you were steaming at such a high speed in thick fog.'

'How do you know we were steaming at speed?'

'It was obvious from the rate of your approach and from the force of the collision. Surely you do not deny it.'

'I deny nothing. I admit nothing. You have a saying, I believe, that it is no use crying over spilt milk. This milk is undoubtedly split and no amount of crying will ever recover it.'

Brett shifted in his chair. The callousness of the man was unbelievable. He seemed perfectly unmoved by the loss of life for which his actions had been, if not entirely, at least to a large extent responsible. Apparently he could pass off the whole affair as no more than a trifling inconvenience; perhaps annoyed at the delay caused to his own ship, or the damage inflicted on her bows. Not that there could have been much damage, for, judging by the pulse of the engines, the ship must again be pushing ahead at something approaching full speed.

'Damn maniacs!' Grill had said. Perhaps Grill was right.

'You have sent out a radio message, of course?'

'A radio message?' Govorov repeated. 'For what purpose, may I ask?'

'I should have thought that was obvious. Surely you have informed other ships of the disaster. Even if you are unwilling to search for survivors yourself, there might be others ready to do so — others more humane.'

Captain Govorov glanced at the man sitting to his left and slightly behind him. This man had not yet spoken a word, and Brett had scarcely noticed him. He was not the kind of man whose appearance draws attention to himself. He was short, squarely-built, and wearing a dark blue suit that did not fit very well. His fair hair was cropped close to his head in the old Prussian style, and he had a round, pudgy face that gave the impression not so much of having been smoothly shaved as of never having had any hair upon it. It was like the face of an overgrown infant, and this impression was accentuated rather than diminished by the large, perfectly round, steel-rimmed spectacles that he wore. The skin was peculiarly colourless, as though it had never been exposed to the sun, or even, for that matter, to the light of day. It had a bloodless, graveyard quality that was strangely repulsive.

He had lost the second finger of his left hand and had a habit of placing that hand over his mouth with the forefinger resting on one cheek and the third finger on the other, so that, glancing at him casually, one had the unpleasant impression that the missing finger had somehow or other been thrust up his nose. He had a small round mouth and astonishingly red lips. His teeth were not good and were almost brown in colour.

'Comrade Linsky,' Govorov said. 'Did you wish to say anything?'

Linsky shook his head; and Brett, examining him more closely, saw that the eyes behind the glasses were cold and passionless as stone. Linsky's voice was high-pitched and squeaky, like an unoiled hinge.

'Go on, Captain, go on.' There was something peremptory in the tone. It was as though this plain, insignificant-looking man had a sense of his own power. He spoke with an air of authority.

Captain Govorov turned again to Brett. 'We have made no signal. Unfortunately at the moment our radio is out of order. Yes — out of order.'

He paused, looking down at the table and drumming on it with his long, delicate fingers. 'We shall, of course, put you ashore when that is possible. I cannot say just how long that will be. Until then you will be allotted a cabin, you and your friend, which I think will be to your liking. Your meals will be brought to you there.'

He glanced again at Linsky, who was holding his face in his left hand, the missing finger apparently lost in the recesses of his nose. Linsky nodded and Govorov went on. 'Yes; it will be best so. If you have any complaints do not hesitate to let me know.'

'I should like to ask when we can expect to be put ashore,' Brett said.

'That is impossible to say with any certainty — quite impossible.'

'But surely you know what your next port of call is.'

'The hazards of the sea,' Govorov said, 'make that always a matter of uncertainty. It is unwise to predict anything.'

Brett Manning was not by nature a very patient young man and this deliberate avoidance of a plain answer to a straightforward question angered him. 'I am simply asking you when you expect to make port.

67

You can answer that. I am aware — too much aware — that unforeseen happenings may cause delays, but there must be an expected place and date of arrival. That is all I am asking you to tell me.'

Again Captain Govorov glanced at the silent man beside him. Linsky's face was expressionless, his eyes staring coldly. Govorov coughed.

'I am sorry. With regard to my ship I can answer nothing.'

Brett felt the colour mounting in his face. He tried to speak calmly. You would get nowhere by shouting at such men as these.

'Captain Govorov, you must see that this is highly inconvenient for us — not to put the matter more strongly. To be left in complete doubt as to our future is quite intolerable.'

'Sometimes it is better not to know the future. He would, moreover, be a brave or a foolhardy man who would forecast it.'

'I am not asking you to play the rôle of a crystal-gazer,' Brett said. 'All I ask is some idea of when I and my friend can hope to return to England.'

Captain Govorov's shoulders went up and down. 'That is more than any man can say.'

Brett's anger rose. He could feel the heat in his face. 'I believe that you are being deliberately evasive — for what purpose, I cannot say; but I warn you that I shall make it my business to report this conduct to the proper quarter at the earliest opportunity. There are such things as laws of international conduct. It seems to me that you have broken quite a number of them tonight. As soon as I get ashore I shall know what to do.'

It was the squeaky voice of Comrade Linsky that broke in, without expression, without any trace of feeling.

'Ah yes, my friend; but when will you get ashore? That is the question, is it not?'

There was silence for a moment. Brett had the feeling that he had somehow stumbled into the middle of a nightmare; there was no sense to be found in it. Grill Butler, bewildered by a language he could not understand, looked questioningly from one to another and scratched his cannon-ball head. And Linsky, his brief speech ended, replaced his left hand over his face and stared coldly from behind the wide circles of his glasses.

Govorov broke the silence. 'And now, gentlemen, I have much work to do, and no doubt you would be glad to sleep.'

He raised his voice suddenly to shout: 'Georgi! Georgi!' and a seaman, who had apparently been standing outside the cabin, opened the door and poked his head inside.

'Show our passengers to their cabin,'

69

Govorov said. 'You know the one.'

The interview was ended, and Brett felt too weary to press further for answers to all the questions he wished to ask. Tomorrow, he thought; tomorrow he would return to the attack.

He rose from his chair and signed to Grill to follow him. Govorov gave a short, jerky nod of the head that might have been a bow. Linsky merely stared at them coldly until they had left the room.

The cabin to which Brett and Grill were conducted by their silent guide was not so luxuriously appointed as that of the captain. Neither was it so large. Two bunks, one above the other, the bedclothes already arranged on them, took up the greater part of one side. There was a wash-basin with hot and cold water taps and a lid that folded down over it to form a small desk, two chairs, a table with fiddles along its edges, a wardrobe, and a looking-glass screwed to one of the bulk-heads. A circular port-hole had been closed to keep out the cold night air and a small steam radiator made the cabin almost too warm for comfort.

The seaman who had shown them the room left immediately, shutting the door behind him. An attempt by Brett to engage him in conversation had failed. The man, morose and stony-faced, replied only with a shake of the head to the questions that Brett put to him.

'Proper clam, ain't he?' Grill remarked when the fellow had gone. 'Did you get any information out of the captain? You were jabbering long enough.'

'Nothing,' Brett said. 'He wouldn't tell me where the ship was bound or how long it was likely to be before we could be put ashore.'

'Damn his eyes! What does he think we are — prisoners of war?'

'I don't know. I've heard about Russians being secretive; but where's the point? Even if he's feeling guilty about what happened I don't see why he shouldn't tell us where we're going. It can't make any difference.'

'And the other little runt; where did he fit in?'

'Comrade Linsky? I don't know that either. He seemed to have some authority over the captain. You noticed how Govorov kept turning to him as if he was asking for advice or seeking approval? That's a queer thing for a captain to do on board his own ship.'

'Seems to me,' Grill said, 'that there's a whole bagful of queer things about this ship. Tomorrow we'll take a look around. Maybe we'll pick up a bit of information then.'

Brett and Grill were awakened in the morning by a small, dapper man with sleek black hair and a pencil-line moustache. He was dressed in blue trousers and a blue steward's jacket buttoned up to the neck, and he spoke Russian in a soft, caressing voice, with an accent that made his words difficult for Brett to understand. He was carrying two towels, a comb, a safety-razor, and a shaving-brush.

'With the compliments of Captain Govorov,' he said. 'The captain trusts you have slept well.'

He went out and returned a few moments later with the clothes that Brett and Grill had been wearing when they came on board.

'These are dry now. I will bring breakfast in one hour. Good?'

'Very good,' Brett said. 'What is your name?'

The steward smiled, and Brett realized that this was the first smile he had seen since coming on board the *Gregory Kotovsky*. It was a very pleasant smile.

'Boyan. Anton Boyan — from the Soviet Republic of Armenia.'

He brought his heels together and bowed from the waist with a little jerky movement like a nodding doll. 'Anything I can do for you I shall be most happy to do.'

'That is very kind of you,' Brett said. 'Thank you.' He looked into the steward's face, noting the liveliness in the jet-black eyes, which perhaps reflected the liveliness of the man's brain, the perfect white teeth that were revealed when he smiled, and the queer little chin that might have been shaped with the help of a grindstone, so extremely sharp and pointed was it.

'You can perhaps tell us where the ship is going and when we are likely to reach port?'

The smile left Boyan's face as though it had been brushed away. He glanced nervously at the door behind him, then back again at Brett.

'No; I cannot tell you that. That is a matter for the captain and officers. I am only a steward. I know nothing of the movements of the ship — nothing whatever.'

He turned quickly and left the cabin as though fearful of any further questions on such a subject.

'There's a funny little devil,' Grill said. 'What made him suddenly take fright?'

'I asked him where we were going. It's like a taboo — something you must never ask.'

'What did he say?'

'Said he was only a steward and didn't know.'

Grill rubbed the bristles on his chin with a noise like the rasping of sandpaper. 'First ship I been in where the blessed stewards didn't know everything. He knew all right.'

'That's what I think. But he was scared to tell. Now, why should that be?'

Grill had lifted the lid of the wash-basin and turned on one of the taps. Steam rose from the basin. 'One thing,' he said, 'the water's hot.'

★ ★ ★

When they had shaved and dressed Brett and Grill went on a journey of exploration. The cabin, which opened on to a narrow alleyway, appeared to be situated on one of the upper decks amidships on the starboard side. They turned left, and having reached the end of the alleyway, found a door which opened out on to a covered deck that must recently have been swabbed down, for it was wet and slippery underfoot.

About six yards from the doorway were rails athwart-ship, with two gaps where the port and starboard companion ladders ran down to the main-deck. Brett and Grill walked to these rails and stood looking down on the after part of the ship — the hatches, the main-mast, the samson-posts, and derricks, the winches and bollards. Between the hatches and the bulwarks were a number of packing-cases, apparently covered with tarred paper, and lashed to the deck with wire ropes secured to iron lugs. Half a dozen men were slouching towards the poop and chanting a rather sad tune. They were wearing greasy quilted jackets that came almost to the knee, and fur-lined caps with the earflaps dangling.

'Don't seem a very sprightly lot,' Grill remarked. 'Look more's if they was going to a funeral than a wedding.' He sniffed the air, filling his lungs with a deep breath and expanding his chest. 'Well, boy, the weather has cleared and that's something to be thankful for. I wonder if there's any other poor devils from the *Silver Tassie* alive. I doubt it; I very much doubt it. No; they'll all be dead. That feller Lock now — I never liked him; you know that; but I wouldn't have wished that lot on to him. He'll be drowned along with the rest. Me and you, we're the only ones left to tell the tale. And we don't even know when there'll be a chance of that — not yet, we don't.'

The fog had certainly cleared; and a fresh breeze was coming out of the north-west, flicking the tops of the waves and touching them with white like so many house decorators' brushes. It was a dull, cold morning, with nowhere a trace of the sun. The sky was leaden and the sea, but for the milk-white crests of the waves, was like a vast expanse of broken slate. There was not another ship in sight.

'Let's have a look at the for'ard end,' Grill said.

They turned and walked along the starboard side between the rails and the wall of the deckhouse, the boat deck forming a roof over their heads, until they came to the forward end of the deck. Here they halted, leaning on the upper rail and gazing down upon the fore-deck. Between the forecastle and the bridge were three hatches, all securely battened down, and on either side of the hatches were half a dozen timber packing-cases similar to those on the afterdeck. Every part of the ship that was visible to them was painted a flat, dull grey; there was not a touch of bright colour anywhere to be seen.

'Like war-time,' Grill said. 'That's how the ships we used to take in convoy were painted. Camouflage, you know. Didn't think there was any painted that way these days. If the hull's the same colour — and I wouldn't mind betting it is — you'd need sharp eyes to pick out this ship at any distance on a day like this.'

'Why do you think a ship would want to be camouflaged in peace-time, a merchant ship?' Brett asked.

'Who knows? Is there any understanding Russians? Maybe they want the ship to move around without being noticed. Anyway, we know something about her now.'

'What do we know?'

'This much,' Grill said. 'That she's flush-decked with five main holds. She's got plenty of accommodation and I'd say at a guess she runs to some seven to eight thousand gross tons and a maximum speed somewhere around the fifteen knot mark. Single smoke-stack, a bit fat and squat with a dinner plate on the top. She's a steamer and probably burns oil fuel. What's more, she can't have taken much harm in the bows from that smack last night or she wouldn't be cracking on speed like she is now; you can feel her shake. Maybe there's special reinforcement up for'ard to tackle pack-ice. If her home port's Archangel she must meet plenty. What more? Well, she's painted grey and heading west for an unknown destination. If I knew what was in them crates down there I might be able to make a few more guesses; but I don't, so I reckon we may as well go and see if that feller Boyan, or whatever his name is, has brought the grub. Damned if I couldn't eat a Russian if he was cooked proper.'

★ ★ ★

After breakfast the two Englishmen received a visit from Comrade Linsky. They heard someone limping along the alleyway and the limping footsteps halted outside the cabin door. There was a sharp knock, then the door opened and Linsky came in.

Brett was surprised to see that he was lame; the previous evening Linsky had been seated during the whole of the interview and his lameness had not been apparent. Now it was obvious that there was something seriously wrong with his right leg. He seemed unable to bend it at the knee, and when he walked the leg swung stiffly from the hip in a half-circle.

'I may come in?'

The question obviously did not call for an answer: Linsky was already in. He closed the door behind him, limped to the table, and sat down in one of the chairs. He took a notebook from his pocket and a ball-pointed pen, opened the book and prepared to write.

'I should like some information, please.

78

Last night you were tired. I did not worry you then. Now perhaps you will be so good as to answer certain questions.'

'What sort of questions?' Brett asked.

Comrade Linsky rubbed his smooth, pallid cheek with the three fingers that remained on his left hand. His eyes peered coldly through the large, round spectacles. He looked like a man whom it would be impossible to rouse to anger, a man who would always retain perfect control over himself and would be just so much the more dangerous for that. The emotions of joy, of love, of pity would surely have been alien to him. Brett could not imagine Linsky ever giving way to such weaknesses; he could imagine the man experiencing hatred, but even then it would be a cold, calculating hatred that would put him in no danger of losing his self-control.

'First, your names in full.'

'Brett Manning and James Henry Butler.'

Brett spelt out the names slowly as Linsky wrote them down in a small, neat hand. Then the Russian looked up at him again.

'Are you Manning or Butler?'

'Manning.'

'Now, the name of your ship.'

'I told Captain Govorov that last night. The *Silver Tassie*.'

'The *Silver Tassie*,' Linsky repeated thoughtfully. 'And what cargo was this ship carrying?'

'I don't see that that has anything to do with you,' Brett answered. 'Why should I provide you with this information?'

The softness of Comrade Linsky's face suddenly appeared to harden, as though the muscles had tightened under the skin; and the moist lips were compressed into a thin line. For a moment he stared into Brett's eyes, saying nothing. A sense of coldness, not of fear but of repulsion, travelled along Brett's spine — the kind of sensation one experiences when the fingers accidentally come upon a toad hiding beneath some garden shrub. He imagined for an instant that Linsky was going to spit venom at him; the fellow was obviously not used to meeting resistance and did not like it. But the venom was controlled; Linsky's face relaxed; even, it seemed, the faintest glimmerings of a smile twitched the corners of his red little mouth. But the smile did not spread to the eyes; the eyes were cold and calculating as ever.

'It is for purposes of record. All must be in order, you understand. I am under instructions from Captain Govorov.'

'Oh; I see.' But Brett did not see. He did not see what concern of Govorov's or Linsky's the cargo of the *Silver Tassie* could

80

possibly be. However, there had been nothing secret about it, and if it would please them he supposed he might as well answer their questions.

'Very well, then,' he said. 'The ship was carrying electrical equipment; though what difference it can make to you or Captain Govorov now that it's all at the bottom of the Arctic Ocean, I fail to understand.'

One way or the other, he thought, it made no difference. Yet he knew that some people were never content without every detail, useless as it might be. The bureaucratic mind had to have everything tidily filed and docketed, as if in such book-keeping lay the solution to every problem — parochial, national, or international. Perhaps the minds of Govorov and Linsky were of this type. He would answer the questions and then he would put some of his own to Comrade Linsky. It would be tit for tat.

'What kind of electrical equipment?'

'Transformers, dynamos, I suppose. I did not see the bill of lading.'

'And for what port were you bound?'

'Archangel.'

Linsky wrote in his notebook; then he looked up again, tapping his ugly teeth with the end of his pen. 'Now, Mr Manning, a personal question. Where did you learn the

Russian language?'

'I learnt it in the Army.'

'Ah, you have been in the British Army, then?'

'I did my National Service. Everyone has to.'

'Just so; just so. And what branch were you in?'

'Intelligence.'

'Yes?' Comrade Linsky's interest seemed to quicken, as though he had at last got something to put his teeth into. A more demonstrative man might have shown excitement; Linsky showed nothing but a certain whiteness of the knuckles as his fingers pressed harder upon the pen. 'And where did you do this work of Intelligence?'

'In Germany — some of the time.'

'Ah!' Linsky's head was bowed again over his notebook. His voice was quite expressionless as he asked: 'Have you ever been in Russia?'

'No.'

'Has your friend?'

Brett translated the question for Grill's benefit.

'I been ashore in Archangel and Murmansk,' Grill said. 'Archangel ain't so bad, but Murmansk's a lousy hole if ever there was one.'

Brett translated the first part of this answer to Linsky but diplomatically omitted the remainder. Grill's personal opinion of the town of Murmansk could hardly be considered essential to the record. Linsky, having noted down the brief facts, returned to his questioning of Brett. From first to last he showed very little interest in Grill Butler.

'Were you a member of the crew of the *Silver Tassie*?'

'No; I was a passenger. Butler was one of the crew.'

'Why were you travelling to Archangel?'

'Does that matter?'

'It is necessary,' Linsky said. 'It must all be recorded. It is necessary for us to give accounts. You must realize that what occurred last night was a serious matter. Anything that has a bearing on it must be recorded — for the proper authorities.' He repeated the last words with great respect in his voice. 'The proper authorities.'

Brett failed to see why the proper authorities, whoever they might be, should be interested in his reasons for going to Archangel, but he thought it best to humour Linsky.

'I was going as representative of my uncle's firm of timber merchants Josiah Manning,

83

Son, and Company. We import timber from Russia.'

'Who were you to see in Archangel?'

'I had a letter of introduction to a Mr Alexander Chernevsky.'

'You have the letter now?'

'No; it was on board the *Silver Tassie*.'

For a moment Brett had the laughable impression that Linsky was going to chide him for being so careless as to leave a valuable document on board a sinking ship. But all he said was:

'You remember the address, perhaps?'

'No; I do not.'

Linsky tapped his teeth. 'You are sure you cannot remember?'

'Quite sure.'

'H'm!' There was obvious doubt in Linsky's mind. He stared at his notebook as though reluctant to leave it uncompleted by the address of Mr Alexander Chernevsky. It was apparent that Linsky had a passion for order: the lack of an address to attach to the name of Chernevsky upset the order of his notebook.

'You cannot remember even the street?'

'Not even that.' Brett was secretly amused by the discomfiture of the cold, crop-headed interrogator. Even if he could have remembered the address he would not have revealed it now.

84

'We will pass on,' Linsky said at last. 'I am not completely satisfied, but we will pass on. Perhaps later the address will come to your mind. This Alexander Chernevsky — what were you going to discuss with him?'

'I am sure I do not know,' Brett said. 'Timber, I suppose. It was more or less a good-will visit.'

'You had perhaps some proposition to make?'

'No; nothing of that sort. My uncle thought it would be good experience for me.'

'Your uncle is a British government official?'

'Not at all, he is a business man. He hates politics.'

'Oh!' Linsky appeared to find this hard to believe. 'How long were you going to stay in Archangel?'

'Just as long as it took to unload and reload the *Silver Tassie*. I was going to use the ship as a hotel and return to England with her.'

Linsky wrote this down and then sat for a while staring at the words in front of him as though he were trying to extract some hidden meaning from them. Then he closed the notebook with a snap and thrust it into an inner pocket of his blue serge jacket. He screwed the cap on his pen and got up.

'Thank you. That will be all for the present. If you remember the address I should be glad if you would let me have it.' He glanced round the cabin with the cold, critical gaze of a man who seldom missed any detail, however small. 'You have no complaints about your food or accommodation?'

'None at all.'

'Good; good.'

'There is one thing, however,' Brett said. 'Now that you have questioned me, I should like to ask you one or two questions before you go.'

'You are at liberty to ask,' Linsky said, stroking his soft, smooth chin with the three fingers of his left hand.

'First, then: when shall we be put ashore, and where?'

Linsky shook his head slowly from side to side like a doll moved by clockwork. 'That is a question I cannot answer.'

'Cannot — or will not?'

'Does it matter which?'

Brett felt as though he were beating his head against a brick wall; always he came up against this refusal to reveal the ship's destination. Someone must know where it was going, but no one would tell. He controlled his anger with an effort. It was necessary to be patient with people like Linsky, difficult as that might be.

'You must understand,' he said, 'that there

are people in England who will be worrying. I have a fiancée, an uncle, other relations: they will all learn that our ship has been lost; if they hear no more they will have to assume that we have been drowned. Do you not see the pain it will cause them? Surely it must be possible to get in touch, to send some message?'

'Captain Govorov told you last night,' Linsky repeated stolidly, 'that our radio is out of order.'

'Then for God's sake put us ashore. Norway cannot be very far away.'

'The ship must not be diverted from its course. We have no orders to go to Norway.'

'But this isn't a question of orders; it's a question of common humanity. Can't you understand that?'

Comrade Linsky slipped the pen into his breast pocket and clipped it there. He showed no more emotion than would have been shown by a recording-machine. Perhaps that was all he was — a machine for recording information.

'The good of the individual,' he said in his high, squeaky voice, 'must always be subservient to the good of the state.'

He turned and went out of the cabin. The interview was over. Brett heard him limping down the alleyway, until the sound of his footsteps was swallowed up in the unceasing beat of the ship's engines that were driving them on and on to a destination that must remain unknown.

'Damn him!' Brett said. 'Damn the little bastard's filthy eyes!'

Grill was sitting on his bunk and picking his teeth with a pin. 'What was all that natter about?' he asked.

'The swine wanted to know all our business, but he wouldn't give away any of theirs. That tale about the radio being out of order. I'm damned if I believe it.'

'What I can't fathom,' Grill said, 'is what that blighter's position is on board this ship. He ain't one of the officers, else he'd be in uniform; they're fond enough of the old gold braid. Likewise, he's no deck hand. He's got too much to say and his paws is too soft.'

'Chief steward?'

'I doubt it. Stewards like to dress up too; that's my experience anyway. Besides, you said yourself that he seemed to have some power over Captain Govorov, and that don't fit in with no steward.'

'Well, whatever he is, he's a nasty piece of work.'

'You're right about that,' Grill said. 'I wouldn't trust him with the kid's money-box; straight, I wouldn't.'

4

Southward

'Four days,' Grill said. 'We been travelling nearly due west. By my reckoning we should soon be getting close to the Greenland coast. If you was to ask me I'd say we was pretty near ready to turn south and come down through the Denmark Straits. That's if Captain Govorov don't intend to land up in Greenland.'

Brett and Grill, from their vantage point amidships, were gazing down upon the fore-deck to where a gang of men were engaged in fitting a new wire rope to the jumbo derrick. According to Grill they were a clumsy lot, but he, having served in the Royal Navy, was inclined to criticize even the best of merchant seamen. 'Not how we'd have done it under the White Ensign,' he would say. 'All wrong; all wrong. But there; what can you expect?'

For two days the *Gregory Kotovsky* had been ploughing her way through rough seas and squalls of sleet and snow; but now the wind had moderated and the seas had gone down. The sky was clear of cloud, but there was a haze like thin gauze, through which the sun, low on the port beam, gleamed coldly, like a bronze coin.

'Me, I'd be glad if we did go south. Get a bit of warmth in the air; get the sun on our backs.'

'I don't mind which way we go as long as we get ashore,' Brett said. 'This is like being a prisoner.'

'A prisoner!' Grill scratched his stomach. 'Maybe that's what you are — and me, too — ruddy prisoners. Prisoners with nothing to do. They feed us but they don't tell us nothing. What are they afraid of?'

'I suppose you didn't find out anything from that seaman? What's his name?'

'Gubin? No, nothing important. They must all have been told not to let on where we're going. Other things, yes; but that, no.'

Grill Butler had encountered Peter Gubin quite by chance on the afterdeck. Grill was examining one of the steam cargo winches and mentally comparing its construction with that of the British equivalent. No restrictions had been put upon the two survivors as to their movements about the ship, and one of the engineers had even conducted Brett round the engine-room, obviously proud of his gleaming machinery.

'Very powerful, comrade; very powerful indeed.' He clenched his fist and tensed his arm in a demonstration of their great strength. 'They would drive a ship even through pack-ice.' He was like a child showing off its pet toy. He had a young, intelligent face, and he seemed to think of nothing but his precious engines, which were the best in the world, really the best in all the world. When, however, Brett sounded him on the question of the ship's destination his face suddenly hardened and he would say nothing. It was the brick wall again.

And it had been the same with Grill Butler and Peter Gubin. Grill, bending down to examine a detail of the winch, had heard a voice behind him and had been startled to recognize undoubted English words, uttered with an accent that was a strange mixture of Cockney and foreign.

''Ullo, mate; 'ow's tricks?'

Grill straightened with a jerk and stared. A very tall, heavily-built man, indeed almost a giant, was grinning at him. The man was wearing the usual fur-lined cap with hanging ear-flaps, greasy quilted jacket, quilted trousers and felt boots. His face was wide in comparison with its length and seemed to be made up of a collection of high, bony promontories thinly covered by leathery, wind-beaten skin. His mouth was a long, straight gash, and his eyes, unlike the dull and sombre eyes of so many of the crew, were bright and sparkling. It was as though an essentially happy and exuberant nature were reflected in them.

Grill looked at him in amazement. 'You speak English?'

'English; yes, I speak it. Not good per'aps. I learn it off a man from London. You know London? I am with 'im in a ship once — a Swede ship; you unnerstan' Swede?'

'Yes, I understand.'

'Joe Smith, 'is name is. We are chinas, see? Long time we are together, an' so 'e learn me 'is language. I speak it not so bad, eh?'

'You speak it fine,' Grill said. 'What's your name?'

'Gubin — Peter Gubin.'

Grill had hurried to tell Brett about this Cockney-taught Russian seaman.

'Thought I was big,' Grill said. 'But he's bigger than me. Not so much meat on him maybe; I fancy I'd beat him on the scales; but he could give me three inches in height and reach. He's young, too; I'd like to take him in hand and make a boxer out of him; he's just right for a heavyweight.'

'How did he learn English?'

'He was in a Scandinavian ship with a

Londoner called Joe Smith. Wanted to know if I knew him. Now I ask you: how many Joe Smiths might there be in eight million Londoners?'

'Perhaps it wouldn't seem so ridiculous to him,' Brett said. 'I suppose when you're a Russian and look at a map of the world Britain must appear pretty small, and London smaller still.'

Grill pulled at one of his thick cauliflower ears. 'Ah, but he ain't Russian — not properly speaking. He comes from Latvia — born in Riga.'

'Oh, one of the poor devils that were swallowed up by the Great Bear.'

'That's right. And somehow I don't think he loves 'em very much.'

'I don't expect he's got much reason to. But he wouldn't tell you anything?'

'Not what I wanted to know. Maybe he couldn't. Maybe they don't tell the crew everything.'

'Or maybe he was scared.'

'Oh, sure; he might have been. As a matter of fact, he sheered off pretty sudden like, and when I looked round there was that slug, Linsky, staring at me. One day I'm going to get my fingers round that bastard's neck, and when I do I won't leave go till he's had it; straight, I won't. What's he always snooping about for? He don't do a hand's turn of work; not what you'd notice.'

'Did he say anything to you?'

'He said something, but I'm damned if I could understand it. It wasn't English.'

Brett pulled one of the cigarettes that Captain Govorov had given him from his pocket and lit it, shielding the match with cupped hands.

'I wonder whether Linsky knows Gubin can speak English.'

'Ah; I wonder.'

★ ★ ★

Grill's forecast of the ship's movements proved to be accurate. Captain Govorov must have given orders for the alteration of course during the night, for when Brett and Grill awoke next morning they discovered that the *Gregory Kotovsky*'s head had been turned towards the south, towards the regions of the sun.

'Maybe we're going to America,' Grill said. 'It'd suit me. I ain't been in New York since the War. I know a nice piece there.' He scratched his head, raising little parallel marks of red on the smooth, tight skin. 'Though maybe,' he added, 'she wouldn't be such a nice piece now. That was twelve year ago.

They don't allus keep that long.'

'If we do hit America there's going to be a load of trouble for Govorov and company when we tell what we know to the right people,' Brett said.

'What do you think they'd do? Would they arrest the Old Man? I'd like to see them arrest Mister flamin' Linsky.'

'I don't know what they'd do; but there is such a thing as international law. The Americans should know all about that, with the United Nations building right there in New York.'

'Sure they ought. And they're the boys for action. They don't altogether love the Russkis.'

It might have been no more than a coincidence, but when the Armenian steward, Boyan, carried in their evening meal he also spoke of America. He asked Brett whether it was true that there were ten thousand millionaires in that country. Brett said he knew there were a lot, but he didn't know exactly how many; and Boyan said yes, he was sure it was ten thousand; he had read it in a book.

Boyan had been born in Erivan, and as a boy he had thought that this must surely be the largest and finest city in all the world, and that Michael Novikov, who was manager of the factory where Anton's father worked and who drove about in a big, black car and drank, so it was said, two bottles of champagne every day, must be by far the richest of men. Then he had heard of America and of millionaires who owned private yachts and as many as ten cars, each one of which was more luxurious than the big, black saloon of Michael Novikov; and at that moment had been born in the ragged, barefoot boy a great and burning desire for wealth and power. America became the Eldorado of his dreams. If only he could somehow get to America, to New York, which was as big as fifty Erivans, he was convinced that he could soon make his fortune.

This was what he told Brett in his soft, eager voice as he stood in the little cabin on board the *Gregory Kotovsky*; these were the hopes and desires that came tumbling from his mobile lips.

'Why don't you emigrate?' Brett asked. 'Why don't you leave Russia?'

'Leave Russia?' Boyan glanced over his shoulder and there was a scared look in his eyes, as though he were afraid of being overheard even mentioning such a terrible thing. 'Ah, it is not so easy as that. It is not easy at all. But America; there would be a fine place to live.'

Then, hurriedly, as if afraid he had already said too much, he added: 'Please; please do not tell anyone what I say to you. Do not tell Comrade Linsky.'

'Why Linsky in particular?'

Boyan seized Brett's arm. 'Because he — because I would not wish him to know that I talk to you about these things. He would not understand — or perhaps he would understand too well. You will promise?'

'Of course I promise. The less I have to do with Comrade Linsky, the better pleased I shall be.'

Boyan sighed with relief. He had been for a moment very tense; now he relaxed. He moved to the door, but as he was about to leave the cabin he turned back.

'Ah, I forgot. There is a message from Captain Govorov. He would like to see you in his cabin this evening.'

★ ★ ★

Brett found Captain Govorov alone. Since the first interview he had seen very little of this man. Occasionally he had caught a glimpse of him in the distance, striding back and forth along the wing of the navigating bridge, a peaked cap pulled down low on his head, the pointed beard jutting out. But

Govorov was not much in evidence about the ship. Orders flowed down from him by way of subordinates, but he himself stayed at the nerve centres — the bridge, the chart-room, his own cabin. He knew how to delegate authority; he was not for ever concerning himself with details that should have been dealt with by lesser men. If there was any worry upon Govorov's mind, it was not the worry of small matters.

He was standing when Brett entered the cabin, and the shortness of his stature was apparent as it had not been when he was sitting. His shoulders were broad, and somehow, when you saw him seated and looked only at the fine, distinguished head, which might have been the head of an artist or a statesman, you gained the impression that he must be tall. In fact, he was no more than five foot six, his legs being short in comparison with the upper part of his body; yet for all this lack of proportion he moved with a certain springy rhythm, like an athlete.

He welcomed Brett in his deep, musical voice and indicated a chair for the Englishman to sit in. He offered cigarettes and Brett accepted one. They were rather unusual cigarettes, half the length being a hollow cardboard tube which acted as a holder for the rest. In the other half was a strong, heavily scented tobacco rolled in rice-paper. The smoke, almost blue in colour, filled the cabin with a strangely exotic odour, that seemed to Brett out of keeping with a plain cargo steamer, but perhaps matched the ornate furnishing of the room.

Govorov opened a cabinet, took out a bottle of vodka and two glasses and placed them on the table. He filled the glasses with the colourless liquid, handed one to Brett, and sat down facing him across the table.

'I hope you are being well looked after,' he said.

'I have no complaints in that respect,' Brett answered.

'But in others perhaps? It is unfortunate, but these things cannot be avoided.' Govorov swallowed his vodka at a gulp and put the glass back on the table. 'I am going to be frank with you and admit that it may be some considerable time before you are able to leave the ship.'

'Then you are not going to America?'

'America!' The word seemed to startle Govorov. 'What gave you the idea that America was to be our destination?'

'It was simply a conjecture based on the observed movements of the ship. First we travel due west for four or five days, then we turn southward and come down through the

Denmark Strait; that is so, isn't it? Why not next another alteration of course to take us to New York or Boston?'

Captain Govorov shook his head. He still had an air of weariness, but he seemed more relaxed than he had been when Linsky was sitting at his side.

'You have been very observant. Perhaps your wishes have fathered your thoughts. But no; I must disappoint you; we are not going to America. Our voyage is to be a long one. I fear that you may not be able to leave the ship until we return to Russia.'

'Russia!' It was Brett's turn to be startled. 'But that is ridiculous. What is to prevent our leaving when you reach your next port of call?'

'That,' said Govorov, 'is a question to which you will find an answer when we get there. I cannot tell you now.'

'And you will send no message to let our friends know that we are safe?'

'The radio — '

'You will forgive me if I say that I do not believe the radio is out of order. It could have been repaired by now.'

Govorov was unmoved. He showed no resentment, no emotion of any kind. 'I am afraid it makes little difference what you think or what you do not think. No message can be sent. You must understand that your presence on board is an embarrassment to me.'

'We had no desire to impose ourselves upon you,' Brett said, 'and we should be glad to leave. It was not our fault that we had to come aboard. I think you will have to admit that.'

A little colour crept into Govorov's pale cheeks; it was evident chiefly upon the high cheekbones. Brett wondered whether it was a flush of shame at the memory of that disaster in the Barents Sea which had undoubtedly been largely the fault of the Russian. Shame, too, for the inhumanity of his behaviour afterwards.

'Nevertheless,' Govorov said, 'you are our guests now and nothing can alter the fact. It is awkward for both sides; but it is a state of affairs that must be accepted. You can make things more comfortable for us and for yourselves by the correct conduct.'

'And what is the correct conduct?'

Captain Govorov drew on his cigarette. His soft brown eyes betrayed a glint which seemed to give evidence of a streak of hardness in his character, of an iron will hidden by the tired, courteous manner.

'During your stay on board,' he said, 'you may see things that will surprise you. Do not seek to inquire too deeply into anything that you see. Do not inquire at all. Do not question any of my seamen — they will tell you nothing, but do not question them. Obey orders.'

'We are prisoners then?'

'I would not put it so.'

'Nevertheless, whether you put it so or not, it is true. We are held against our will; therefore, we are prisoners. Well, at the moment there is nothing we can do to alter the situation; we are in your hands; but I warn you, Captain Govorov, when the time comes you will have much to answer for. Do not forget that.'

'I will not forget. But when will that time come?' He got up and took Brett's empty glass. 'Now, another vodka.' His voice was pleasant. It was as though he had thrust all that was disagreeable firmly behind him. He was now the charming host entertaining an esteemed passenger. 'Let us have no more talk of prisoners. You are my guest. Do you care for music?'

The question was so unexpected that for a moment Brett was at a loss to answer. Then he said: 'Yes; I like it very much.'

'Then you shall hear some of my records. I have a very good selection.' Govorov was smiling; the glint had gone from his eyes; the iron was hidden. He filled Brett's glass and then took a portable gramophone from a cupboard. It was an electrical machine of a type that Brett had not seen before. Govorov plugged the lead into a socket near the floor of the cabin and took some records from a rack in the cupboard that had obviously been specially constructed to protect them from any damage that might have been caused by the rolling of the ship. Handling them gently with his delicate fingers, as a connoisseur might handle precious china, he placed them on the table.

'These are mainly operatic,' he said. 'The human voice has always fascinated me. I think it is the most beautiful of all musical instruments. There is no other that has the same range, the same flexibility, the same power to rouse the emotions. Do you not think so?'

He had become suddenly enthusiastic, as a man does when he speaks of something in which he is intensely interested. He slipped one of the discs from its cardboard container and put it on the turntable.

'This is Chaliapin — perhaps the greatest of them all.'

It was an aria from *Boris Godunov*, and the portable gramophone reproduced it amazingly well. The great voice seemed to fill the cabin as though the man himself were there and not dead long ago. Govorov sat back in his chair, his eyes half closed, his whole mind given to Mussorgsky's music, and this, its finest interpreter. When the record came to an end he seemed to wake from a dream, to require an effort to bring his spirit back from wherever it had travelled on the wings of the song. His voice when he spoke held a tinge of sadness, of regret for what was lost in the past and could never truly be recaptured.

'I saw him once; in Milan, not in Russia — he left after the revolution and did not return. I shall never forget it. No one who has seen Chaliapin could forget. He had a presence — I cannot describe it; it was the power in him; he held you. It was as if he had but to stretch out his hand and beckon, and you were his, body and soul you were his. And yet he was only a peasant. Perhaps that was the secret; perhaps it was because his roots were in the soil of Russia that he could sing for her, for the great plains and forests, the rivers and the hills. He was her son.'

'And yet he left her.'

'Yes,' said Govorov slowly; 'he left her.'

He got up and changed the record.

He played many more records, choosing them himself, not asking Brett whether he liked this one or that; perhaps believing that what he liked Brett must surely like also. He seemed to have recordings of all the great basses, of Kipnis, Pinza, Christov; but few tenors. Possibly the tenor voice was not manly enough for his taste. He had some orchestral records too, but chiefly it was the bass voice and the music of Russian composers, of Borodin, Glinka, Tchaikovsky, Mussorgsky, and Rimsky-Korsakov.

Finally he put the gramophone away, and asked Brett whether he played chess.

'I have played it a little,' Brett said.

'You will have a game with me?'

'I shall be pleased to.'

Govorov took from a drawer in the table a board inlaid with ivory and ebony squares. The pieces also were of ivory and ebony. It was a beautiful set, magnificently carved, and Brett voiced his admiration. Govorov seemed pleased.

'I have had it many years. It was my father's. We used to play, he and I — ' He paused, as though having caught himself in a weakness, and did not go on. Instead he said briskly: 'But no more of that. Will you take white?'

Govorov mated in six moves. It was the same in the second game. Brett was outclassed and knew it. Govorov was too polite to remark on this wide divergence of skill; but though Brett was to hear the records again on several occasions Govorov never again suggested chess. They were far too unevenly matched to make the game enjoyable for either player.

When he left the captain's cabin Brett encountered Comrade Linsky. Linsky's smooth, lard-like face was as expressionless as ever and his eyes peered coldly from behind the steel-rimmed glasses. Brett thought for a moment that Linsky was going to question him, perhaps to inquire the reason for his visit to Captain Govorov. But he did not do so; he merely gave his stiff, jerky little nod of the head that was more insulting than another man's sneer, opened the door of Govorov's cabin without troubling to knock, and limped inside.

Brett went back to his own cabin more puzzled and disquieted than he had been since coming on board. The mystery of the *Gregory Kotovsky* seemed deeper than ever.

Grill was waiting for him, eager for news. 'Well, did you get any sense out of the Old Man?'

'Nothing. He played gramophone records to me and told me how much he admired Chaliapin.'

'Who in hell's Chaliapin?'

'He may not be in that place even though

he's dead. He was a singer.'

'A singer! Was that all you done — talk about singers?'

'We played chess. The captain's a good player; he knows too many moves for me.'

'To hell with chess! Didn't he tell you anything?'

'He told me we were in for a long voyage and that it would be advisable to behave ourselves.'

'I'll behave meself. I'll tear this ruddy ship apart.' Grill was striding about the cabin, clenching and unclenching his massive fists, his battered face red with fury and frustration. 'What's he think we are? We're Englishmen. He can't treat us like we don't matter a tinker's damn. We're free men, ain't we?'

'At the moment I hardly think we are. I'm afraid we shall just have to bide our time.'

Grill sat down heavily on one of the chairs, which creaked under his weight. 'All right, then. If we must we must. But the time'll come; and when it does I'm going to get my hands round somebody's neck, see if I don't.' He picked up a towel and began twisting it in his fingers as if practising the art of strangulation. 'I ain't forgot my mates aboard the old *Silver Tassie*. Somebody's got to pay for that job some time.'

★　★　★

The following day Brett was coming out of the lavatory, which was situated a short distance from the cabin he shared with Grill Butler, when he almost collided with a boyish-looking officer carrying a handful of papers. The man apologized politely and was about to pass on his way, when an idea seemed to occur to him.

'You can read Russian?' he asked.

Brett said that he could, and the officer took one of the folded sheets from under his arm.

'This is our ship's newspaper. Perhaps you would like to have a copy.'

Brett, rather surprised, accepted the sheet and glanced at it. It was in typescript, and had obviously been run off on a duplicator. It was headed: *The Gregory Kotovsky News*.

The young officer smiled. 'I see you are surprised that we have a newspaper; we produce it for the benefit of the crew. I am on my way to deliver it. It is good to have a newspaper on board ship, do you not think so?' He was evidently very proud of this amenity. 'Just like the big liners, eh?'

'But how do you receive the news?' Brett asked.

108

'By radio, how else? I am the second radio officer.'

'Oh; and can you send out messages also?'

'But of course.' The young man smiled again. He spoke patiently, as though he were dealing with a backward child who had never heard of the wonders of science, and did not understand how messages could be sent from ship to shore and vice versa. 'You do not suppose that we are ever out of touch with Moscow?'

'Then you have repaired the radio?'

'Repaired it? Why do you say that? There has not been any need for repair.'

'But surely it has been out of order.'

The officer seemed puzzled; his forehead wrinkled. 'Out of order? No; not at all. What can have given you that impression?' He appeared to take the suggestion as a reflection on his own efficiency. 'Our radio is always in first-class order. It is essential that we keep it so. The ship's engines may break down, yes; but the radio, never.'

'But I thought — ' Brett began, and then stopped. There was no point in telling this friendly young man what Govorov and Linsky had said. He knew now what he had already guessed: that there was no technical reason why a signal should not have been sent out, that it was of set purpose that the disaster in the Barents Sea had not been reported. And yet, perhaps it had been reported — to Moscow. It was obvious from what the radio officer had said that the ship had never been out of touch with Russia, no doubt in code. Perhaps it was from there that orders had come to proceed from the scene with all speed.

Brett was surprised that neither Linsky nor Govorov had taken the trouble to brief the radio officers concerning this matter. Perhaps it had never occurred to them that he might learn the truth from such a quarter.

He found the young Russian — he was little more than a boy — gazing at him curiously.

'Yes? You thought something — ?'

'Nothing. It was a mistake. Thank you for the newspaper, I shall enjoy reading it.'

'You will find everything of importance recorded,' said the radio officer. 'I think you will have to admit we make a very good journal with our little printing-press.'

He moved off down the alleyway and Brett returned to his cabin. Grill saw the paper and was at once interested.

'What you got there, boy?'

'Ship's newspaper,' Brett said. 'The second Sparks gave it to me. Seems they do a regular printing. He gave me an interesting bit of information, too; something that isn't printed here. He said the radio had never been out of order.'

Grill rubbed his cheek reflectively. 'Oho! So it was all lies.'

'Exactly.'

'What you going to do? Tell the Old Man what you've heard?'

'I don't think so. It would only get the Sparks into trouble and it wouldn't help us. We guessed it was all moonshine anyway, didn't we? Well, if they wouldn't send a signal before, they're not likely to do so now just because we happen to know they can. Still, it does show us where we stand.'

Grill was looking at the news-sheet. 'What's it say in there? Anything about ships being sunk on the way to Russia?'

'I doubt it,' Brett said. 'I'll read it to you.'

Neither of them gained much satisfaction from *The Gregory Kotovsky News*. It was very efficiently censored. There was a rather lengthy report of a speech by a high party member, a tirade against deviationists, and some blasts at Tito. There were figures of output from a number of factories which had exceeded their quota; a report, heavily biased, of Communist activities in Malaya; an attack, quoted from *Pravda*, on United States policy in the Far East with particular reference to

Formosa, Korea, and Chiang Kai-Shek; and unimportant snippets of local news from certain obscure Russian towns and villages, which were possibly the homes of various members of the crew. A surprisingly large amount of space was devoted to sport, quite half a page reporting progress in a chess tournament.

'Chess!' Grill said disgustedly. 'Who's interested in chess?'

'Apparently they are.' Brett folded the paper and threw it on the table. 'Well, there it is; that's the lot. I don't think we'll take out a subscription to this rag.'

★ ★ ★

Day followed day, and still the *Gregory Kotovsky* drove steadily southward. The sun stood higher in the sky; the air grew warmer; and Boyan brought clothes more suitable for tropical weather than the thick clothing in which Brett and Grill had come on board.

'Captain Govorov says you will be more comfortable in these,' Boyan said. 'If they do not fit I will change them.'

There were blue cotton trousers and shirts of the same material and colour. Brett thanked the little steward, and he and Grill tried on the clothes while Boyan waited.

Brett's were a reasonably good fit, but Grill could not force his bulk into the trousers offered to him.

Brett laughed. 'You'll have to go on a diet. They're feeding you too well.'

Boyan was staring in fascination at the tattoo revealed on Grill's bare chest — the shell-damaged Eiffel Tower and the record of his unfortunate love affair with Gladys. Brett translated the words for him and Boyan grinned.

'This Gladys; what kind of a girl is she? Is she big and strong and ugly like him?'

'I should hardly think that possible, but I cannot say; I never had the pleasure of meeting her.'

'What's he saying?' Grill asked suspiciously.

'He's interested in Gladys,' Brett said. 'Wants to know if she was as pretty as you.'

'Tell him to go to hell,' Grill said. 'Tell him to wipe that grin off his kisser and fetch me a bigger suit.'

Boyan went willingly enough and came back with a pair of trousers so enormous that even Grill's swelling stomach was lost inside them.

'They'll do,' Grill said. 'I can take in a reef or two.' Boyan seemed inclined to linger. He came back to the subject that obsessed his mind — America, the United States. Brett felt that if he had told Boyan that the streets of New York were paved with gold and the skyscrapers studded with diamonds the steward would have believed him. But there was no need to go to such lengths; to tell the unvarnished truth — that thousands of American factory workers went to work daily in their own cars, that the American working man had in his house such luxuries as refrigerators, television sets, washing-machines, and every other labour-saving device, and that the emigrant from Europe could rise from poverty to riches in a few years: these simple facts were enough to make Boyan's black eyes glow like coals and his white teeth gleam in a smile of joy.

'It is true then? True? It can be done? A man can become a millionaire in that country?'

'Oh yes; it can certainly be done; it has been done. But not everybody who goes to America becomes rich. There are poor people there too.'

Boyan brushed this fact aside as though it were not worthy of his consideration. 'If I went there I should become rich.' Then he sighed and his shoulders drooped in a theatrical gesture of despair. 'Ah, but how to get there — how?'

'Surely there must be some way if you wish to go there so much.' Brett felt sympathetic.

He liked Boyan, who was so different from the other stolid Russians. Boyan with his black hair and eyes, his trim black moustache, and his flashing smile, was like a piece of quicksilver compared with the lead of the others.

Boyan said eagerly: 'Tell me how I can. Tell me.' Suddenly he stopped speaking and appeared to be listening. Brett listened also and heard the sound of footsteps approaching down the alleyway, limping footsteps. Boyan left the cabin hurriedly and as he went out Comrade Linsky limped past. Linsky did not look into the cabin; he did not even look at the steward, but Brett had the uncomfortable feeling that Linsky's pale eyes had missed nothing. It occurred to him that Linsky was for ever moving about the decks and alleyways with his limping tread, and that whatever went on in the ship Linsky knew about it. And again he wondered what was the precise position of that enigmatical character of whom everyone, from the captain downward, seemed to walk in fear.

★ ★ ★

It was strange how few other ships were ever sighted from the *Gregory Kotovsky*. Occasionally a smudge of smoke would be visible in the distance, sometimes a vessel hull down on the horizon; but few ever approached at all closely. Brett wondered whether Captain Govorov purposely avoided the main shipping lanes, purposely avoided speaking to other ships. For days together the lonely ocean stretched away on all sides, unmarked by mast or sail or funnel, a vast desert of loneliness across which the vessel ploughed her solitary way — southward, ever southward.

Often, now that the weather was so hot and the cabin almost unbearably so, Brett and Grill would lie out on deck stripped to the waist, and the strange decoration of Grill's chest would occasion interest even in the Russian seamen, who for the main part treated the survivors with indifference. Grill basked in this interest, rather enjoying it. It seemed to give him a feeling of superiority.

'Peter Gubin arst what the words was,' Grill said. 'He can't read English. Seems like his shipmates had been discussing it among themselves.'

'What did you tell him?' Brett asked.

'I told him the tower was a naval decoration for bravery and the words meant 'Awarded by My Lords of the Admiralty'.'

'And crossed out again for bad conduct, I suppose. Did Gubin believe that?'

'He never said he didn't.' Grill laughed for a while, his belly shaking, savouring his own little joke. Then he became serious. 'That Gubin's a decent feller. I don't believe he's got much love for Russians. Well, would you have if they'd pinched your country? He told me there's a couple more Latvians aboard — pals of his.'

'You seem to have talked to him a lot.'

'Not much, really. I think he's scared to be seen having too much to do with me. It's usually a hole an' corner business when there's nobody else about. It's always like he feels he's being spied on — if you know what I mean.'

'I know — Linsky.'

'Him and maybe others. This ain't like a British ship, not by a long chalk. There's too much damned mystery about it. I'd like to have a look at that cargo.'

'You'd better not. If they catch you prying about there may be trouble. We've got to be patient, Grill, just patient, and wait for an opportunity. This ship must make a landfall some time; she can't go on sailing and sailing for ever. When she does, then perhaps we can do something.'

'When she does,' Grill said, 'they'll have a job to hold us. They'll need to put us in irons.'

'They might do that. They might even do that.'

5

A Rendezvous

The *Gregory Kotovsky* did not pause in her southward run. Any idea that her destination might be somewhere in Central America was dispelled when she crossed the Tropic of Cancer and bore southward still towards the Equator, driving on through the hot, calm days and the warm, starry nights with undeviating and inscrutable purpose.

'Brazil maybe,' Grill said. 'I wouldn't mind a dose of Rio or Santos.'

But it was not to be. The Pole Star faded out of the sky like a lamp extinguished, and ahead shone the Southern Cross, and the days became cooler; and still the ship's head pointed like an arrow towards the south.

'Maybe we've hit a ruddy Antarctic expedition,' Grill suggested. 'Maybe there's motor sledges in them crates. You and me, boy, we'll be hiking to the South Pole afore we know where we are. What price me as Captain Scott and you as Titus Oates?'

He and Brett were sitting in their cabin and the steam heater was going again. Grill, to pass the time, had taken to manufacturing rope sandals with the help of a palm and needle which had been in his pocket when he came on board. Gubin had supplied the rope and thread.

'By the time we get home,' Grill said, 'I'll be able to stock a shop. That's if the rope don't give out.'

He was remarkably handy with a needle. 'You learn to be in the Navy.' And he had already traded a dozen pairs of sandals with members of the crew in exchange for tobacco, using Peter Gubin as middle-man. But he grumbled about the quality of the leaf. 'It ain't like the stuff I been used to smoking. Proper horse dung. Reckon they mix a bit of oakum in with it.'

Brett was reading a book that Captain Govorov had lent him. It was a novel by some modern Russian author, very much of the Communist school. It was full of party propaganda, but beneath the overlay of work norms and labour heroes there was an absorbing thread of narrative. The man might have written a good story if he had not been hampered by ideological restrictions.

Govorov had offered the book with a half-satirical smile twisting his sensitive lips. 'Read it and see what is coming out of Gogol's overcoat these days.'

Grill had a look at it and put it down in disgust. 'Don't see how you can make head or tail of that stuff: Not but what it's lucky you can. We don't know much as it is, but we'd know a sight less if we had to rely on Peter Gubin as an interpreter.'

He pushed the triangular-shaped needle into the shoe he was working on, thrusting it home with the little metal disc in the palm of his hand. 'Hell, I wish something would happen. This is a fine game played slow. Enough to drive a man crazy.'

It was half an hour later that Brett suddenly looked up from his book.

'Listen,' he said. 'Notice anything?'

Grill paused in his sewing and cocked an ear. Then he nodded. 'Sure, sure. Something is happening now, I do believe.'

The regular beat of the ship's engines that had scarcely altered its rhythm for weeks had changed to a slower tempo.

Grill flung his shoemaking equipment on the table and jumped to his feet. 'We're slowing down, boy, slowing down. Now what's that for? There wasn't no land in sight when I was up on deck an hour ago, and by my reckoning there ain't no land hereabouts, not for miles.'

Brett closed his book with a snap. 'I'm going to have a look. You coming?'

'You bet I am.'

Brett opened the cabin door and was about to step out into the alleyway when he came suddenly face to face with a Russian seaman.

'Go back!' It was not a request; it was an order.

The man's voice was harsh. Round his waist was buckled a cartridge belt and at his hip swung a holster, the black butt of a revolver showing. He put his hand on the butt with an action of warning that could not be mistaken.

Brett stood in the doorway, moving neither back nor forward. 'I wish to go on deck. You have no right to stop me.'

The seaman was unmoved. His granite face showed no flicker of emotion. 'It is forbidden.'

'Forbidden? Why?'

'Captain Govorov's orders. You must stay in your cabin until other orders are given.'

'But that is ridiculous. You cannot keep us shut up. You have no right.'

'Orders,' the seaman repeated stolidly. He eased the revolver a little way out of its holster. 'Do not make trouble.' There was a note of menace in his voice. 'I warn you, do not make trouble.'

Brett had the uncomfortable feeling that this man would not hesitate to shoot to enforce obedience. He did not look intelligent, and perhaps he was all the more dangerous for that. There was an air of brutality about him; he had a cruel mouth and small eyes. The fingers resting on the butt of the revolver were covered with the innumerable scars that are seen on the fingers of men who use them for hard manual toil. The nails were black and broken.

Grill was impatiently breathing down Brett's neck.

'What's the hold-up? What's he talking about?'

Brett answered without turning. 'He says Captain Govorov has given orders that we are not to leave the cabin.'

'To hell with that for a tale. I'm coming out. This mug can't stop us.'

'Wait,' Brett said. 'The man's armed and he looks ready to shoot if there's any trouble. We'd better think this over.'

He pushed Grill back into the cabin and closed the door.

'Come and sit down. No sense in being hasty; we've got plenty of time.'

Reluctantly, Grill allowed himself to be persuaded, grumbling all the time. 'I could have kicked that plug-ugly out of the road. I could have dealt with him.'

'No need for that yet,' Brett said. 'Wait a

little. Listen to the engines.'

The engines were still beating at the slower rate; there was scarcely any vibration.

'Dead slow, I'd reckon,' Grill said. 'What's the reason, I wonder? What's the reason?'

'Wait. We shall see.'

They waited. Outside the cabin they could hear the guard shuffling his feet and coughing. They heard someone else go by in the alleyway, say a few words to the guard, and receive a brief answer. He laughed abruptly as though some joke had been made. Then there was a series of muffled thuds which might have been caused by the guard kicking his heels against the wall of the alleyway. Another man went past, singing softly to himself. The engines continued to beat.

Suddenly the ship vibrated as though a surge of fear had passed through it. The door of the wardrobe began to rattle madly.

'Putting 'em in reverse,' Grill said. 'That'll be to take the way off her. We're coming to a stop.'

As suddenly as it had started the vibration ceased, and the door of the wardrobe was quiet again. There was no longer any sound from the engines.

There was a sudden rush of feet along the deck outside. A man shouted. Then the

Gregory Kotovsky bumped against something solid, not heavily, but just hard enough to send a shiver through her that could be felt in the cabin.

There was more shouting, another rush of feet, and the rattle of a steam winch being started.

Brett unscrewed the wing-nuts of the port-hole and swung the glass back on its hinges. He put his head out, but could see nothing beyond the ship's rails but a wide expanse of grey water, heaving gently in long, shallow undulations.

'Anything there?' Grill asked.

'Nothing on this side except sea. No land. Nothing.' He stepped back from the port-hole and Grill had a look. 'You know what it is,' Grill said, pulling his head in again. 'There's only one thing it can be — another ship on the port side. That's what the bump was; that's what the winches are going for — making her fast.'

He began pacing about the cabin in scarcely controlled excitement, unable to keep still.

'This may be our chance, Brett. We got to make use of it. Cooped up here, damn it, cooped up here! What do they think they're doing? Prisoners — that's what we are. Putting an armed guard on the door, of all things. It's — it's against the law; it's illegal.'

'Perhaps they don't worry too much about legality. They've already done a few things that mightn't bear looking into.'

Suddenly Grill came to a halt. 'I'm going to take a look at that ship,' he said, 'and nobody's going to stop me — gun or no gun. Who knows? She might be British or Yankee. She might be able to give us a passage home; and here we are shut up in a stinking little cabin just because it pleases his lordship, Govorov — or that toad, Linsky. Well, I'm not standing for that, not me. Are you game?'

'I'm game,' Brett said. 'I don't intend to miss this chance. But how about the fellow outside?'

'I'll look after him,' Grill said. 'You leave him to me.' They could hear no sound in the alleyway. The guard had stopped kicking his heels, and no doubt everyone else had gone out on deck to look at the other ship.

Grill lifted his finger. 'Now quiet, boy; quietly does it.' He moved to the door, tip-toeing with surprising lightness for one of his massive build. He turned the handle very gently; then with a sudden, rapid movement he pulled the door open and leaped out.

If the guard had been standing close to the door things would have been easy for Grill, but the man had shifted some distance up the alleyway. Grill lost a valuable few seconds looking for him in the wrong direction, and in that time the man was able to pull his revolver from its holster. As Grill turned and lunged at him he fired hurriedly, jerking the gun in his haste. The bullet whined past Grill's ear and went ricocheting like an angry bee down the length of the alleyway.

Grill's fist took the Russian in the throat. He choked and the gun fell from his hand, skidding along the floor of the alleyway almost to Brett's feet. Brett stooped and picked it up.

Grill hit the guard again, this time on the point of the jaw, very hard. The man's head jerked back like the head of a puppet and struck a row of rivets in the wall of the alleyway. His eyes became dull and filmy. He slumped to the floor and lay still.

'Come on, boy,' Grill said. 'Time to go.' They turned and ran down the alleyway.

Brett was first through the doorway. The chilly air met him as he stepped into the open, and it was like taking a plunge into cold water. He shivered.

It was a grey day with a blanket of cloud, and rain coming in brief showers, and the afterdeck on which Brett and Grill looked down glistened with moisture; it had a cold, steely appearance.

Brett did not pause to contemplate this view; he ran to the port rails and saw at once that their guess had been correct: there was indeed a ship made fast alongside. He could hear the fend-offs groaning under the pressure as the two vessels moved uneasily upon the swell, rubbing against each other like two great animals.

The decks of the second ship were low fore and aft, almost at water level, studded with tank hatches and ventilators and overlaid with a maze of pipes. The thick, squat funnel was aft, and between forecastle and bridge, bridge and poop, stretched high cat-walks. The entire ship, like the *Gregory Kotovsky*, was painted a dull slate-grey.

Grill came to a halt beside Brett, staring down at the other vessel on whose fore-deck a gang of men were busily hauling at a long flexible pipe.

'A tanker,' he said. 'Can you beat that? We're going to refuel.'

Brett did not stay to brood on this discovery. Whatever happened he had to make contact with someone in authority on board this other ship, an officer. It was the only chance. He had to hurry.

With the revolver still clutched in his right hand he ran along the deck until he was level with the bridge of the tanker. He saw an officer on the wing of the bridge and shouted across to him in English, hoping that he would understand that language.

'What ship is that? What nationality? We are English, English. We need help. We are being held against our will.'

His words rushed out almost incoherently and, slowly petered away into silence. The officer looked at him without a flicker of understanding on his face; he simply looked puzzled.

Brett pointed to himself. 'Inglese, Inglese.' Then he felt Grill's hand on his arm and heard Grill's hoarse voice full of disgust.

'No good, boy; no good at all. Look there.'

Grill was pointing to the stern of the tanker, and following the direction of his pointing finger, Brett saw fluttering languidly from its staff the ship's ensign. It was a red flag with a hammer and sickle and a star in one corner.

'Russian,' Grill said. 'Another bloody Russian. No help for us there.'

At that moment Brett felt a numbing blow on the right wrist and the revolver fell from his grasp. He spun round to find four seamen and Comrade Linsky facing him. There was a flicker of a smile on Linsky's lips, but it was not a pleasant smile.

'We will go back to our cabin now,' he said. 'We have had our little game.'

Captain Govorov was angry, and the iron was showing through the courteous exterior. Comrade Linsky was sitting in his usual place, on one side and a little behind the captain. Brett and Grill faced them across the cabin table. It was like the first night all over again; but with a difference.

'You have disobeyed my orders,' Captain Govorov said. His voice was harsh.

'We do not recognize your authority to give us orders,' Brett answered. 'We are on board your ship through no fault or desire of our own. Supposedly we are free men.'

Linsky repeated softly the word 'supposedly', as though savouring its taste upon his tongue. Then he covered his mouth with his three-fingered left hand and stared fixedly at the two Englishmen.

'Do you not realize,' Govorov said, 'that the master of a ship has authority to give orders to anyone in that ship while at sea?'

Brett shook his head. 'I do not believe there is any law which gives him the right to confine passengers to their cabins, and to place an armed guard outside the door with orders to shoot if necessary.'

'The law of force, perhaps,' suggested Comrade Linsky.

Captain Govorov said hastily, as though wishing to cover up Linsky's remark: 'You attacked my seaman and caused him a serious head injury. He was entitled to defend himself.'

Grill wrinkled his forehead. 'What's he saying?'

'He says you injured the guard.'

Grill looked at the knuckles of his right hand from which the skin had been torn away. 'I meant to injure him. You can tell these gentlemen I'll injure anyone else what gets in my way. I'm warning 'em.'

Captain Govorov began speaking again; some of the anger had gone out of his voice; he seemed only tired and rather sad.

'You have been treated well on board my ship,' he said. 'Do not abuse my kindness. Believe me, I have it in my power to make things very far from pleasant for you. True, as you have said, you did not come on board quite of your own free will; but your presence is none of my desiring either. We can all make things easier for one another in a difficult situation by behaving in a civilized manner. I ask you to accept the truth of my statement when I say that any orders I may make concerning your movements are for your good as well as my own.' The voice hardened a little. 'I take it that you wish to live?'

'I see no reason why we should not live,' Brett said.

Captain Govorov sighed. 'There are a great number of things that perhaps you do not see. There are also many things that it is better you do not see. Men have often died because they knew too much. Better to know nothing and live than to know too much and die.'

'Am I to understand that you are threatening us?' Brett asked.

'There is no need for me to threaten,' Govorov said. 'I am offering you advice; that is all. You would do well to accept it.'

Suddenly Linsky's squeaky voice broke in. 'It might be wise not to forget that to the world you are already dead.'

Brett was to ponder on this remark later as he lay on his bunk staring at the painted iron above him. Coupling it with what Govorov had said, there could be no doubt at all that he and Grill had received a warning. They would need to be careful. There was no sense in running one's head against a brick wall.

Moreover, as they had left Govorov's cabin Brett had distinctly heard Linsky say: 'Why waste time? Why not finish this matter now?' There was a note of impatience in Linsky's voice, but Govorov had answered: 'No,

Comrade, it cannot be done like that. I will not do it.'

What could not be done? What would Govorov not do? There was a word, was there not — liquidation? It sounded so much less repulsive than murder, yet it was the same thing.

'To the world you are already dead,' Linsky had said. Brett could not avoid the disquieting thought that, if it were left to Comrade Linsky to decide, they would be dead in fact. It was not a pleasant reflection to sleep on.

Nevertheless, on the following day as the *Gregory Kotovsky* once again pursued her solitary way southward, everything appeared to be back to normal. No further restrictions were imposed upon the Englishmen and they were allowed to move about the ship as before.

But there was a difference in the attitude of the crew. It was perhaps that they resented the treatment of their shipmate whose skull had suffered from Grill's rough handling. Where before they had been simply indifferent, now their glances seemed to show active dislike — even hatred.

Peter Gubin had no hatred, but he feared his shipmates. He told Grill that it was no longer safe for him to be seen talking to the Englishman.

'You 'it 'im too 'ard,' Gubin said. 'You cut 'is 'ead open an' it bleed; very much it bleed. So they no like you no more.'

Not that Gubin worried about the seaman's cut head. Grill told Brett that in his opinion Peter was secretly rather pleased. It did not make him sad that one of the Russians had suffered. But he had to live with them, and there was the rub. He had to look to himself.

'Not but what,' Grill said, 'I reckon he's still got some scheme up his sleeve, something he'd like to tell me about if he dared. Maybe he'll come out with it one of these days. He asked me once if we had any plans for escaping. I asked him how he thought we could do that from a ship in the middle of the ocean. He just said there was ways. Wouldn't say any more though.' Grill scratched his stomach. 'This is a queer ship and no mistake. Me, I'd be glad to see the back of it.'

The attitude of Boyan, the Armenian steward, towards the Englishmen had undergone no change. Or if it had, it was simply to take on a deeper respect. Boyan, like many physically underdeveloped men, was impressed by brute strength such as that displayed by Grill Butler, and admired him for his attack on the guard. Boyan, a man apart from the deck crew, and one whose duties made it necessary for him to have continual contact with the two unwilling and unwanted passengers, was not affected by the feelings of the rest of the seamen. Like Gubin and the other two Latvians, Boyan was no true Russian; he had no strong patriotic feelings for the nation of which he was a member simply through the accident of having been born in that particular part of Armenia which happened to be engulfed by the Union of Soviet Socialist Republics. Spiritually Boyan was a whole-hearted capitalist. He desired wealth as some men desire power and others desire knowledge. Again and again he would return to the theme of America and the riches he might make if only he could somehow manage to set his feet upon that precious soil. To Boyan the stars of the American flag were lodestars and the stripes were veins of pure and unadulterated gold.

So Boyan still supplied the needs of Brett and Grill, and, with one ear always cocked for the sound of Linsky's limping tread, spoke freely of his dreams and his desires, of his hopes and of his fears.

Brett liked the Armenian and wished he could have seen some way of helping him to attain his ambition. But, unable to help himself, there was little hope of helping anyone else. There was nothing to do but wait in patience as the *Gregory Kotovsky* slipped deeper and deeper into those chilly waters that ring the coldest of all the continents of the world, the white and frozen continent of the Antarctic.

6

Landfall

The *Gregory Kotovsky* had made her landfall at last. And what a land it was! A bare, lifeless rock, set in a waste of grey and troubled water.

'Land ho!' Grill said. But he said it softly, derisively; gazing away beyond the bows of the ship towards this barren peak of some underwater mountain, this desert island of the south that welcomed them with no golden beaches, no waving trees, no green pasture; but with a grey, petrified face, warning them to keep away, for their own safety to keep away.

And yet it was towards this dreary place that the ship was undoubtedly heading. There was enough activity on the deck and on the forecastle to convince Brett and Grill that this was indeed the end of the long voyage from the far north, a voyage that had taken them down the length of the globe, unbroken save for the one brief halt to refuel. Yet even without the evidence of that activity they would have known by the fever of expectation that had been in the very atmosphere of the ship, the almost palpable tremor of excitement running through her like a current of electricity, that at last they were coming to the end of the journey.

'Land ho!' Grill said again.

The weather was cloudy and cold, with a wind blustering out of the west and chopping up the sea into white-crested hillocks. It was the southern summer, the season of long days and brief nights, and there was no haze to obscure the island. As the *Gregory Kotovsky* approached from the north, drawing closer and closer, Brett could see that what had at first appeared as a single amorphous mass was in fact a line of peaks like the humps on the back of a stegosaurus.

'Nice place for a climbing holiday,' Brett observed. From a jutting promontory in the centre of the northern shore the coast receded southward on either side, sharply to the east, more gently to the west. And to the west the ridge of hills sloped gradually down, in nicely graduated and diminishing height, to a long, low finger of rock which itself ended in a reef stretching for perhaps half a mile farther westward, a maze of jagged and broken teeth through which the sea dashed angrily in a seething cauldron of foam.

'Healthy,' Grill muttered. 'Damned healthy

on a thick night. You get in among that little lot and you've had it almighty quick, and no missing.'

'Surely this can't be it,' Brett said. 'There's no safe anchorage here. There isn't even an inlet.'

Grill massaged his nose, and that mis-shapen blob quivered under this rough handling like a piece of india-rubber. The sound of his wheezy breathing altered in pitch as one nostril and then the other was affected by this treatment. It was like tuneless primitive music being fingered out of some barbaric wind instrument.

'I always did think Russians was mad, boy. Now I know. Nobody but a madman would bring a ship to a place like this. It's about as fertile as a slab of concrete, judging by the look of it.'

But the *Gregory Kotovsky* steamed purposefully on, not directly for the northern shore of the island, but bearing away to the east so that the land was on her starboard side, and soon the promontory had blotted out the view of that deadly reef to westward.

'At least,' Grill said, 'the Old Man don't intend to run her on them little tintacks.'

As they came closer to the shore they could see how the bare hills climbed almost sheer from the water's edge to a maximum height of perhaps three hundred feet, so steeply that it would have taken an expert mountaineer to scale them. Alternate strata of lighter and darker rock, like the filling of a sandwich cake, imparted a striped appearance to the hills. In places narrow, precipitous gulleys reached down towards the sea, marked in clear white lines by snow, which, shaded here from the heat of the sun, had survived from winter.

Peter Gubin came running up the ladder from the foredeck and Grill moved to intercept him.

'Hey! What's this island, for God's sake?'

Gubin cast a hasty look round to make sure that no one else was within earshot, and muttered: 'It is Grinkov's Tomb; Grinkov's Tomb, no other. That is 'ow you say in English.'

He spoke the name with a touch of awe in his voice, as though the bleak, forsaken island had pressed a cold finger on his spirits. Then he tore himself free from Grill's hand and hurried away.

'Grinkov's Tomb,' Brett repeated. 'Grinkov's Tomb. That's a strange name for an island. Ever heard of it, Grill?'

Grill stroked his chin reflectively. He seemed to be thinking back over the years of his sea-going life, searching through his memory of discussions in ships' forecastles, of information passed from one seaman to another, of experiences, good and bad, that this man or that had had. When he answered his eyes were gazing at the island and not at Brett. In his voice, too, there seemed to be a trace of that awe with which Gubin had spoken the name.

'Yes, boy; I've heard tell of it. I've heard of ghost ships and lights where there shouldn't be no lights and voices coming out of the sea and great birds like evil spirits. And I've heard of Grinkov's Tomb.'

'What have you heard?'

'I've heard it's a bad place for ships to come — bad as hell. There's many that have had their bottoms ripped out on that reef over on the other side of the island, and never a one that had any good from it. They say the reef's haunted; haunted by Grinkov.'

'Well, who was Grinkov?'

'A Jonah, boy; a Russian and a Jonah. I'll tell you how it was according to the way I heard it. This Grinkov was a seaman on board of a Yankee whaler, 'way back in the sailing days. I suppose he'd gone out to America to make his fortune, or something, and shipped aboard the whaler because he couldn't get a job ashore. Or maybe he liked the sea; I don't know. It didn't like him, that's certain.'

'Go on.'

'Well, there he was mixed up with a tough Yankee crew on board the *Cyrus Brilling*, if I've got the name right. It was something like that anyway; and the *Cyrus Brilling* was an unlucky ship. Trouble mounted on trouble: the captain died of a fever, the cook ran amuck and carved up the second mate with a meat axe, the water went bad, they lost the mainmast in a gale and they didn't sight no whales. Fifteen months they'd been at sea and not a barrel of oil to show for it. No wonder they was sick. The crew wanted to turn for home, back to Nantucket, but the new captain wouldn't hear of it. No oil, no money, see?

'They'd tried the Pacific, and then they came back round Cape Horn and drove eastward. It was no better, storms nearly all the way and no whales. The crew grumbled; what crews don't? They looked around for a Jonah to blame it all on to, and of course there was this poor devil Grinkov what couldn't hardly speak English. Who else could it be that was bringing the bad luck?

'Then one day, in the worst gale of the lot, they came out of a squall of sleet to find themselves driving straight for this here

141

island, straight on to the rocks. It seemed as if nothing could save them, so what do they do? They lay hold of this blighter Grinkov and pitch him overboard, and that's the last of him.'

'What happened after that?'

'The tale goes that as soon as they'd got rid of the Russian their luck changed. They missed the rocks by a miracle, the weather improved, and two days later they fell in with a school of right whales. In no time at all they'd got their barrels full of oil and were on their way home.'

'So it looked as if Grinkov was a Jonah.'

Grill nodded. 'You might say so. Anyway, that's how the island came to be called Grinkov's Tomb. It's been the tomb of a good many others since then. That's why they say he haunts the place. They say he can make storms to drive ships on to the reef so that he can have companions. It's a lonesome sort of grave to have all to yourself.'

'You don't believe that part of the tale, do you?'

'At sea I don't disbelieve anything. It ain't safe to. All I know is that no seaman would willingly come near the place and no captain would risk his ship within twenty miles of it if he wasn't forced.'

'Except Govorov.'

Grill shook his head slowly from side to side. 'Govorov's a Russian. All Russians is mad. And maybe Grinkov treats them different, seeing they're his countrymen.'

The wind lost some of its force and the sea became smoother as the *Gregory Kotovsky* came under the lee of the island. Here on the eastern side the coast was slightly less precipitous than on the northern, but there was no sign of an inlet, and nothing that might have suggested a beach on which a boat's crew could have made a landing; nothing but the barrier of rocky cliffs on which could be seen no trace of vegetation, except here and there a suggestion of green that might have been moss or lichen.

For perhaps a mile and a half the ship ran southward along the eastern shore at reduced speed. Then she heeled over in a sharp turn to starboard and headed straight for the island, as though intending to ram the unyielding rock and force an entrance by sheer strength.

'Madness,' Grill muttered gloomily. 'I told you so. What's old Govorov think he's playing at?'

But it soon became evident that Govorov knew very well what he was doing. The ship rounded a headland, and there to the north was a narrow opening between the cliffs.

'So that's it,' Brett said. 'There is an inlet.'

It was indeed an inlet, though a very narrow one, being scarcely more than a ship's length across; and it was situated between a long, curving peninsula of rock that came down the eastern side of the island like a finger, and the main mass of the island itself. On either side the cliffs rose steeply like rock walls, and between was a strip of smooth water. Into this strip, with consummate skill, Captain Govorov eased his ship. From more than a cable's length away it was almost invisible, the cliffs blending with one another to give an appearance of complete solidarity, and few captains would have ventured so close in the hope of finding an entry. But Govorov must have known of its existence, must have known that the channel was deep and safe, for he had not hesitated to take his ship straight towards the opening.

'It's a marvel,' Grill muttered in amazement. 'It's a ruddy marvel. You could sail round and round the island for a month and never know it was there.'

'It's like a fjord,' Brett said. 'I suppose it'll be deep enough.'

'Oh, sure, sure. The way them hills slip sheer down into the water, I reckon there'll be fathoms to spare. But where's it lead to? That's what I'd like to know.'

The *Gregory Kotovsky* went straight for the gap, and it was like going into a narrow alleyway between two high walls. The rock cliffs on either side rose to a height that dwarfed the vessel's masts, and as she progressed the channel widened, curving gradually away to the left. In a few minutes the bottle-neck outlet to the sea had vanished astern and the ship was hidden as completely as if the land had swallowed her. She was in fact floating smoothly in towards the very heart of the island.

For about a mile the vessel followed the sheltered, rock enclosed channel, and then suddenly she was in more open water, for the channel broadened into a lake some two-thirds of a mile long by half a mile wide. The ring of hills around it were like battlements shielding it from the wind and hiding it from the sea. It was indeed a perfect land-locked anchorage, a secret harbour which no storm could trouble.

'Can you beat that?' Grill said. 'Who'd have thought there was this snug little haven inside of that rock?'

'Maybe Grinkov's ghost found it and told the Russians.'

'Ay; maybe it did. I'll wager nobody else knows.'

'You'd be pretty safe. When they've got

things like those hidden away they aren't likely to spread the news far and wide.'

Brett was pointing towards the northern shore of the lake. Grill followed the direction of his pointing finger and let out a long whistle of amazement.

'Subs, by God! Now we are learning something. It's a Russian submarine base.'

'Exactly.'

There were twelve submarines, moored in threes, close in under the cliff, their long dark hulls and conning-towers merging with the dark water of the lake below and the dark shadow of the rock above. They looked strangely sinister, as though lying there in wait for some master hand to bring them to life, some master player to set them moving upon the vast chessboard of the oceans.

'A submarine base in the heart of the Southern Ocean. My God — wouldn't the Admiralty like to know about this!'

'And the Yanks. They'd have ten thousand fits.'

Suddenly the anchor chain started to rattle out through the starboard hawse-pipe in a cloud of red rust. Steam rose from the windlass, a bell clanged, and the ship came to rest, swinging to her cable like a dog chained to its kennel.

'Well, we're here,' Grill said. 'This is it.

This is what we been wanting to know — and much good may it do us now we do know. No need to ask no more what's in them packing-cases, nor in the holds neither. As sure as my name's James Butler they're base stores, torpedoes, ammunition, and what have you.'

He stroked his chin and his ugly, battered face was grim. When he spoke his voice held a more serious note than Brett had ever heard. Usually it was hoarsely cheerful or hoarsely angry; now it was frankly worried.

'You and me, boy, we seem to have put our heads into it proper. Who'd have thought we'd have jumped on board a ruddy Bolshie supply ship?'

He paused. His forehead was puckered. He seemed to be pondering the implications of what he had seen.

'I wonder how this is going to affect us?'

Brett suddenly remembered a remark that Captain Govorov had made, something about men having died because they knew too much. Well, he and Grill knew too much now. There was here a top secret of top secrets. Indeed, it was more than disquieting that they had been allowed to see so much. When the *Gregory Kotovsky* had gone alongside the tanker to refuel an attempt had been made to confine them to their cabin; now, when there was so much more to see, they were allowed to move freely about the ship, to observe and note. For that there could surely be only one reason — a certainty on the part of the Russians that this knowledge would never be imparted to anyone else, that the men who knew too much would never be allowed to talk.

He touched Grill's arm and indicated with a sweep of his hand the long, dark shapes of the submarines.

'That looks bad for us.'

'How d'you mean — bad?'

'Do you think they're going to let the news of this get around? What kind of men tell no tales, Grill? Can you answer that?'

Grill stared at him. 'You don't think they'd do us in? Not like that. Not in cold blood. It wouldn't be human. It ain't our fault we've seen this. We didn't ask to come.'

'I don't think it much matters whose fault it is. It's the fact that matters. When they've gone to the trouble of making a base like this they aren't likely to stop at a little thing like a man's life to keep it secret.'

'I don't believe it,' Grill said, but there was no real conviction in his voice. 'If they was going to kill us, why haven't they done it already? They've had plenty of chance.'

'Govorov.'

'Govorov? Then you think — '

'I don't know. I think if it had been left to Comrade Linsky we should not be here now. Govorov's a different type. He's a mixture. I don't altogether understand him; but somehow I think we owe our lives to him. On the other hand, he hasn't let us go. We're prisoners.'

'Do you think they're likely to keep us here?'

'They might; but in my opinion it's unlikely. Captain Govorov said we'd go ashore in Russia. I'm thinking he may have been right. The question is, what happens after that?'

Below them on the fore-deck the crew were feverishly at work stripping off the hatch covers and rigging the derricks.

'Getting ready to unload,' Brett said. 'They don't waste time. You were right about the stores, I'd say. But how does a ship discharge her cargo in a place like this?'

Grill pointed towards the head of the anchorage. 'That looks like your answer.'

The longitudinal axis of the lake was approximately on the line of east to west. At the head, the western shore, it curved in a wide arc, and here the rocky hills, instead of dropping sheer to the water's edge, appeared to end in a narrow, gently sloping beach.

149

Down this beach was descending a line of strangely flat-topped vehicles, that from the distance looked like barges on wheels. One by one they moved to the edge of the water, took to it like boats and came in line astern towards the ship.

'Amphibians.'

'Right in one,' Grill said. 'Good old ducks. But where did they spring from? They seemed to come out of the side of the hill.'

'From caves,' suggested Brett. 'Natural — or man-made.'

Grill was shading his eyes. 'It's damned hard to see. If only I had some binoculars. Might be caves — and they might be man-made, as you say. I'll believe anything after this lot.'

'If they've dug out tunnels for storage and living-quarters,' Brett said thoughtfully, 'they may have done the same for the submarines. Along those cliffs over there, for instance.' He pointed towards the northern shore of the lake where the rock came sheer to the water, putting it in deep shadow. 'Might be openings along there. Just the place for submarine pens. No need for reinforced concrete. They could slink inside and you wouldn't be able to see a thing from the air, even if you knew what you were looking for. You've got the most perfect camouflage here that you could possibly have.'

Suddenly he heard a squeaky voice immediately behind him, the voice of Comrade Linsky.

'You find it interesting, perhaps.'

Brett swung round. Linsky was wearing a black astrakhan hat and a long coat with an astrakhan collar. The black seemed to accentuate the unhealthy pallor of his smooth, hairless face. His steel-rimmed spectacles were brightly polished.

'You have asked so often what our destination was to be. Now you have the answer. It all comes in good time, does it not? Patience is all one requires.'

He paused, staring at Brett, his mouth twitching slightly, as though he would have liked to smile but would not allow himself that indulgence.

'This is Grinkov's Tomb. A pleasant name, do you not think so? Or perhaps you find it a little sinister.'

The smile asserted itself, wintry as the snow in the shadowed crevices of the hills.

'This island is not in the usual line of shipping. Perhaps you have gathered that. The truth is that ships avoid it at all times. Fortunately for us, the reef has an evil reputation. Stories have grown up around it;

151

you may have heard some of them. Strange how such tales gain credence among sailors; a superstitious tribe at the best of times. The fact that there is a safe anchorage inside the rock is not well known. It is scarcely known at all. It is not the kind of information we should like to be spread abroad. The reason you will, no doubt, be able to figure out for yourself if you have not already done so. I give you credit for not being altogether stupid.'

He gazed a moment at the approaching amphibians, then gave his stiff little nod and limped into the deckhouse. Grill watched him go with an expression of disgust on his face. He made a rude gesture with two fingers at Linsky's receding back.

'What was he talking about?'

'He said the Russians wouldn't like the news about this place to get around.'

'He did, then? A hint, I suppose.'

'Perhaps more than a hint. It sounded to me very much like a threat.'

Grill banged his fist on the rail he was leaning against. 'I'd like to know where Mr flaming Linsky comes into this set-up. I'd certainly like to know that.'

'So would I,' said Brett. 'But we shall know. I have a feeling we shall know all too well before we've finished with him.'

By this time the amphibians had reached the ship. They were bigger than DUKWs and they were manned by men in naval uniform. Quickly and efficiently they were made fast to the *Gregory Kotovsky*, three on one side and three on the other. Two officers stepped out of the leading boat and climbed the accommodation ladder to the deck where Captain Govorov was waiting to greet them. Then the three disappeared in the direction of the bridge.

'Brains-trust,' Grill muttered sarcastically. 'Going to split a bottle of vodka in the Old Man's cabin.'

'Plenty of brass about them,' Brett remarked.

Grill nodded. 'Oh, sure. Top-rankers all right.'

The winches were already clattering, loads swinging up and over the side. Not a moment had been wasted.

Grill voiced his grudging admiration. 'They get down to it quick enough; you've got to say that for them. If they was English dockies they'd still be thinking about it, wondering where to start; that's if they hadn't knocked off for a cuppa.'

The packing-cases on the deck were the first to go, one to each amphibian. Then the first of the strange, ungainly looking boats

153

cast off and headed back for the beach.

'Let's keep an eye on that boy,' Brett said. 'See where he goes.'

They watched the leading amphibian pushing its blunt prow through the water, saw it pause at the edge of the beach, then drive slowly up the slope. In another minute it had disappeared into the blank face of the rock.

Grill thumped his fist on the rail again. 'What did I say? Right slap into the side of the hill. That's where the store is. I'd give something to look inside.'

'They're not likely to give you that pleasure,' Brett said drily. 'They may be proud of their construction, but not so proud.'

Grill was striding backward and forward, quivering with excitement.

'You know what this means, don't you? It means they've got a base just where it can do most harm. If there was a war they could strike at all the shipping going round the Cape. They wouldn't need to bring their subs home. They could service them here. Can't you imagine what Jerry would have given for something like this in the last war? It'd have been worth a packet of ships.'

'Exactly. And that's why you can bet your bottom dollar that the Russians aren't going to let us spread the glad news. We're in a fix,

Grill. We're in the biggest damn fix we could be in, and I don't see how we're going to get out of it.'

★ ★ ★

It was evening when Boyan came to Brett's cabin, though it was still broad daylight.

'You are requested to go to Captain Govorov's cabin.' Boyan spoke in a rather awed tone.

'Is it anything important?'

'Most important,' Boyan said. 'The admiral is here.'

'Admiral! What admiral?'

'Admiral Fedorenko,' Boyan said, lowering his voice, as though he scarcely dared to sully such an illustrious name by allowing it to pass his unworthy lips. 'Admiral Fedorenko is commandant of the island.'

'In that case, I had better go.'

'It would be best.'

Brett found the admiral seated at Govorov's table in Govorov's favourite chair. Govorov was on one side of him and the faithful Linsky was seated in his usual place a little to the rear. Fedorenko was a plump, clean-shaven man with thick, curling hair that was completely white, although he did not appear to be more than fifty years old. His eyebrows, in startling contrast to his hair, were jet black, meeting across the bridge of a wide nose that looked as though it had at some time or other been broken. His eyes also were black. His face had a yellowish tinge and was deeply pockmarked, so that it gave the impression of having been made from pigskin, like an expensive wallet. There was a hint of ruthlessness about the tight-lipped mouth.

'Sit down.'

It was an order rather than an invitation. Fedorenko looked like a man who was in the habit of giving orders and having them obeyed. At this moment he did not look pleased. He was wearing a high-necked tunic of blue cloth, with brass buttons; there were four stars on each epaulette, and over the left breast pocket were three rows of medal ribbons. His heavy chin bulged over the collar in two thick rolls of flesh.

'I should like you to tell me exactly how you come to be on board this ship,' said Fedorenko without preamble.

Brett glanced at Govorov. The captain looked more weary than ever. He had perhaps been having a trying interview with the admiral.

'I should have thought,' Brett said, 'that Captain Govorov would have already told you.'

'What Captain Govorov has or has not told me is not the point,' said Fedorenko sharply. 'I wish to hear your own story.'

Brett shrugged. 'Very well, then.'

He gave it straight, not mincing his words. He wanted Fedorenko to understand that it was criminal carelessness on the part of the Russians that had been the cause of the disaster to the *Silver Tassie*.

'No search was made for survivors. Nothing at all was done. It was a shameful piece of work.'

He thought he saw Govorov wince, but he did not intend to spare the man. Fedorenko's black eyes stared at him unwaveringly.

'How did you manage to climb on board this ship?'

'Somebody lowered a rope ladder over the side.'

Fedorenko turned to Govorov. His voice was harsh. 'Who lowered that ladder?'

'A seaman named Gubin.'

'Ah!' Fedorenko seemed to be engraving the name Gubin on his memory. He turned again to Brett.

'How is it that you understand the Russian language?'

That question again. Patiently Brett explained; patiently he answered again all the questions that Linsky had asked.

157

Suddenly Fedorenko turned once more to Govorov. His voice was hard and the words came snapping out like bullets from a machine-gun.

'Captain Govorov, you have acted foolishly. This matter could have been settled long ago. It ought to have been settled. I must say you have shown very little initiative. Now it must be left to Moscow.'

Brett saw the ghost of a smile flicker across Linsky's smooth face. Then it settled back into its usual cast, without expression, without warmth or colour.

Govorov flushed angrily, stung by the rebuke. He had been spoken to as though he were a backward child, and he did not relish the experience. He drew himself up.

'I am a ship's captain, not, thank God, a politician. I have done enough. There are limits beyond which I cannot, I will not, be forced.'

Fedorenko's voice was smooth again; it almost purred. 'You forget, captain, that it is never possible to do enough for the state. Let us hope that you remember it in future — for your own sake.'

Govorov's hands tightened upon the arms of his chair. He seemed about to answer back, but he restrained himself with an obvious effort. He simply looked at Fedorenko with an expression of contempt in his brown eyes, as though the admiral, in all but rank, were so far beneath him as scarcely to merit consideration. To Brett, the superiority of Govorov as a man over both Fedorenko and Linsky was very evident. They were coarse, earthy creatures, but Govorov was of finer metal. There was an air of fastidiousness about him that seemed to cut him off from his companions like an invisible fence. One could not imagine his sharing with them a single common interest beyond the strict limits of his duty.

Brett now began to return Fedorenko's fire, putting his own questions to the admiral. He wished to know what it was proposed to do with him and Butler. When could they expect to return home?

'You have no right to hold us. We are British citizens.'

'Mr Manning,' Fedorenko broke in; 'I pay you the compliment of supposing that you are not a fool. You have used your eyes. You cannot honestly believe that this is simply a matter of your own personal convenience.' He looked into Brett's face with his keen black eyes. 'No; I see that you understand. It is, I think, unnecessary for me to say more.'

His gaze moved to Govorov, and with a jerk of the head he managed to include Linsky.

'This is a matter for Moscow. It cannot be settled here.'

He gave Brett a sharp little nod of dismissal. 'Very well, Mr Manning. That is all.'

Brett got up and left the room.

In his own cabin he found Grill back on the job of sandal-making. He looked up as Brett came in, his needle poised, his eyes questioning.

'They been hauling torpedoes out of number four hold — dozens of 'em. You didn't think we was sitting on stuff like that, did you? There's what look like cases of shells an' all. Boy, they're setting this place up proper. Did you find out anything?'

'Only that it seems they've decided not to deal with us here. We're to be sent back to Russia. The powers that be in Moscow are to decide what to do with us.'

'Well, that's some consolation, anyway. This place may have suited old Grinkov as a tomb, but personally I'd rather be buried some-where a bit nearer home.'

'Like Siberia?'

'Ah, come off it. We've a long way to go afore we get there.' He clenched his fist and grinned. It was a savage kind of grin, as though he were contemplating some pleasant act of violence. 'A lot may happen on the voyage back. Somebody may even get hurt. *I* don't intend to go to bloody Russia, for one.'

'Nor I for another,' Brett said. 'We'll think of something.'

He felt better for Grill's cheerful savagery. There was something strangely reassuring in the plug-ugly face and bald cannonball head, in the long, thick arms, and great stomach of the man. If it came to rough play Grill was the boy to have on your side.

As Grill had said, it was a long way to Russia. They would think of something. It was a relief to know that they were not to die here.

7

The Plan

On the following day Brett saw three of the submarines moving towards the sheer rock face on the north side of the anchorage. A few minutes later all three had disappeared through what Brett could now just distinguish as an arched opening, like the doorway of a cathedral. So closely did it blend with the dark colour of the rock that anyone not aware of its existence could easily have overlooked it.

This was confirmation of Brett's theory: there were submarine pens inside the living rock; and possibly workshops, a system of dry-docking, everything necessary for an efficient base. And it must be a base of considerable importance to warrant a full admiral as commandant.

During the succeeding days and weeks the weather remained fine. Often the sky was a cloudless blue, but it was always cold where the ship lay, in the long shadow of the hills. The water was calm and unruffled, but often, looking towards the western peaks, Brett could see a plume of fine snow being blown eastward by the wind, so that it seemed as though the peaks were smoking. He could hear the wind, too, whining incessantly as the hills broke its force. It set up a high-pitched, wavering note, that came to be accepted as the musical background to the long listless days.

Only one incident of note occurred during the period of unloading. It happened midway through the afternoon of the fifth day, and caused the only unforeseen stoppage of work.

Grill and Brett were taking a turn on deck to exercise their legs when Grill stopped suddenly and remarked: 'Some feller's having a climb.'

He was pointing towards the foremast, that sprouted up from the deck below them like a great bare pine-tree. Brett looked also, and saw that a man was almost half-way up the iron ladder fixed to the mast and was climbing rapidly.

'Going to do something to the rigging maybe,' Grill suggested. 'Sooner him than me. I'm not the kiddo for heights these days. Too much weight. But that boy can certainly move on a ladder. Proper monkey.'

Brett noticed that one or two of the workers in the holds and on the winches had seen the man, and were gazing up at him as

163

though interested in his actions. He did not pause, but climbed steadily up until he came to the crow's-nest, a little platform surrounded by an iron shield, rather like a small metal tub attached to the mast.

It was when he was standing in the crow's-nest that the man's actions became peculiar. Until then he had been no more than an ordinary sailor climbing a ship's mast, a figure of no particular interest. But having reached that elevated position he suddenly flung wide his arms like a priest bestowing a blessing, and gave three shouts in such a powerful voice that they could be heard even above the clatter of unloading.

If the shouts were intended to draw attention to himself, they succeeded in their object: everyone looked up towards the crow's-nest. Immediately he saw that he was being watched, and having, as it were, thrust himself into the limelight, the man began to act as though a fit of madness had seized him. First he stood upon his hands in that narrow space high above the deck and waved his legs in the air; then he climbed out of the enclosure and hung by one hand from the rim of the shield; and finally he crooked his legs over the rim and hung for a full minute head-downward. In the process his fur hat came off and floated down thirty or forty feet to the deck below. At any moment it seemed the man might follow it.

'He's crazy,' Grill said. 'He'll kill hisself afore he's done. What in hell's he think he's up to?'

It was indeed a hair-raising exhibition that would not have disgraced a circus, and it had the effect of stopping all work in the business of unloading for a space of five minutes. The winches ceased to clatter, the slings were motionless, and everyone was idle, staring upward in fascination at this madman who was risking his neck to provide so unexpected an entertainment.

Then, as suddenly as it had started, the exhibition was over. The man stood for a moment in the crow's-nest, gave a mock bow, and descended to the deck. Brett saw one of the ship's officers meet him at the foot of the mast, put a hand on his shoulder and apparently say something to him. Then the officer walked away and the man followed. In another minute work had started again and everything was back to normal.

Brett turned to Grill. 'Well, what do you make of that? Is this sort of thing a common occurrence on board ships?'

Grill scratched his chin. 'First time I've seen anything like it. I've known some crazy devils in my time, but I've never seen a man hang upside-down from a crow's-nest until now.'

'Seemed as if he wanted to attract attention.'

'He did that all right. He had everybody looking at him. I don't mind telling you it made me sweat just to see him.'

'I wonder whether that was the idea — to get people looking up.'

'Where would be the point in it? I think he was just mad — like the rest of 'em. There's no accounting for what Russians will do.'

'He didn't look mad when he came down. He followed the officer calmly enough. Could you see who it was?'

'Not me. He was too far away.'

It was Boyan who told Brett later that the man was one of the Latvians.

'Josef Slowacki, it was. He used to be in a circus one time. I think he was keeping in practice.'

'But why do it at that moment?'

Boyan shrugged. 'Who knows? Perhaps he wished to make a sensation.'

'Well, he succeeded in that. Will he be punished?'

'He has been reprimanded. It will go down against him. I think they will do nothing else.'

The incident passed like a ripple on the surface of the water and was forgotten. The

166

unloading of the *Gregory Kotovsky* proceeded without pause. More uniformed sailors came out in the amphibians to assist the crew, and had it not been for shortage of amphibians the ship might well have been discharged within a week. As it was, however, there were many periods when the winches and derricks were enforcedly idle. The half-dozen amphibians that had originally come out to the ship apparently composed the full complement of which the base was possessed, and this was not a sufficiently great number to keep the chain going without a break.

Nevertheless, in spite of delays, within little more than a fortnight the holds had been emptied of their cargo and the ship was standing high out of the water.

'She'll want some ballast now,' Grill said. 'No doubt she's equipped with sea-water tanks for that job; they'll be pumping it in.'

But it was soon apparent that the *Gregory Kotovsky* was to have solid ballast as well for the long, and possibly stormy, passage home. Out from the shore came the amphibians, loaded with broken rock.

'Looks like some of the stuff they blasted out of the tunnels,' Brett remarked. 'They must have done a lot of work inside their ant-heap, even if there were natural caves to start with.'

The broken rock was awkward material to handle. There were no mechanical grabs such as might have been used in a well-equipped port, and it all had to be loaded manually into big iron buckets, which were lowered over the ship's side by means of the derricks. Many of the rock fragments were too big to shovel and had to be lifted into the buckets by hand; all of them were particularly resistant to shovel work, and Brett and Grill watched with a certain malicious delight as the Russian sailors heaved and sweated at their labour.

'I don't know how much of that stuff they aim to bring aboard,' Grill said, 'but at this rate I reckon it'll take them a good week to load five hundred tons.'

'Are you in a hurry?' Brett asked.

'A hurry? I d'know. I get the itch, hanging about here. I want to be doing something. I ain't never been the one for idling.'

'You'll just have to be patient.'

'Patient! Dammit, ain't I been patient? How many weeks is it since we hauled aboard this rotten, stinking ship? I've lost count. I've been patient, haven't I? But it's all bottled up, all bottled up, I tell you. One day the cork's going to come out — and that'll be the day.'

A week later the *Gregory Kotovsky* set sail on the long journey home — from the far south to the far north. Admiral Fedorenko came on board an hour before sailing time, attended by another officer with a dispatch-case under his arm. They came out from the shore in a small amphibian that had not been used for unloading, with the white ensign of the Russian Navy fluttering from its stern; but they did not stay long.

Half an hour after they had gone the *Gregory Kotovsky*'s anchor was being dragged up from the floor of the harbour, and the engines that had been silent for three weeks came suddenly to life again.

The *Gregory Kotovsky* did not fly the Blue Peter, for there were no passengers ashore to warn of her imminent departure; but silently, her mission accomplished, she moved away down the channel and through the bottle-neck to the open sea. Half an hour later Grinkov's Tomb was no more than a vague dark shape astern; within an hour it had disappeared from sight behind a curtain of mist.

'And if I never see the place again,' Grill said, 'it'll be plenty soon enough. But wouldn't our people in Whitehall like to know about it? Wouldn't they just?'

'Or the Americans,' Brett said. 'It would

give them something to think about. And of course it's just that fact which is going to make our dear hosts reluctant to see the back of us.'

Grill rubbed his hands together. 'We'll think of something. Now we're at sea we'll think of some way out.'

But three days later, as he and Brett paced backward and forward across the after part of the boat deck, they still had not thought of anything. Or rather they had thought of many things, many ways of escape, and all hopeless.

Three days had passed since their departure from Grinkov's Tomb — three days of steady steaming northward, with the sun coming up on the starboard side and the Southern Cross glittering nightly in the sky astern; and still there seemed to be no way out.

Brett pointed westward. 'Over there is South America; it's a long swim.' He turned and pointed to the east. 'Over there may be Africa if we've reached that far north yet. Either way it must be about a thousand miles. That really is some swim.'

Grill was pulling at his ear, as if trying to ring bells in his head. 'If we could seize the ship — take over control — '

'Two of us against forty or fifty Russians!

170

Think of something else. That horse won't run.'

'It was just an idea. We might get hold of the captain and force him to give the right orders. We could maybe seize the bridge and hold the rest of 'em off from there.'

'Without any weapons? Besides, if we did seize Govorov we probably couldn't make him give the orders; and if he did the others wouldn't obey. You've got to reckon with Linsky for one.'

'I could kill Mister Linsky. It'd be a pleasure.'

'It's no good, Grill; not that way. There are too many of them and too few of us. We'll have to think up some other plan.'

But it was easier to say think of a plan than it was to do so. It is simple enough to leave a ship at sea, the simplest thing in the world. All you have to do is to step overboard. What is not so simple is to find a means of saving your life after having done so. Certain death in the sea was even less pleasant to contemplate than possible death in Russia. What was required was some method of getting away which brought with it at least a hope of survival, and the attempt to think of such a method was to keep Brett awake on his bunk for long into the night.

There were the boats; always his mind

seemed to come back to the boats. They, surely, were for the purpose of saving lives. But, having got as far as thinking of the boats, the insuperable difficulties that stood in the way even of getting one safely into the water presented themselves to him with overwhelming force.

In order to be able successfully to launch a boat it would be necessary to bring the ship to a stop. You could not simply fling a boat into the sea, jump in and let go — especially when there were only two of you to carry out the task. And even supposing it were possible to do so, how could it be done without attracting the attention of the crew, of the officer on the bridge, of anyone who might be awake? For a ship does not sleep, even at night; there are always some of her officers and crew awake and alert.

Thus, if everything else were conceded, if two men could creep up to one of the boats, lower it away and get into it while it was leaping and dancing in the stream of the ship; even given darkness and a calm night; even then it was foolish to suppose the job could be done undetected. And even though they were to get away thus, it would be only a matter of time before they were recaptured. The ship would hunt them down; they could not hope to escape.

Brett toyed with the idea of a raft. At different points about the ship were life-saving floats. Supposing he and Grill were to fling one into the sea during the night, jump overboard and swim to it. It might be possible to do that much without detection. But even so, granted it were done successfully and that the ship did not come hunting for them in the morning, what hope had they of saving their lives in that manner? Drifting on a tiny float in the middle of the ocean without food or water, without protection from sun or wind or storm, they would not be likely to survive for long.

No, it would have to be some other way. Yet, what other way was there? What more effective prison than a ship? He turned restlessly on his bunk, thinking of ways and rejecting them all as hopeless.

Suddenly he heard the handle of the cabin door being stealthily turned. Then a pale gleam of light from the alleyway outside shone into the cabin, a narrow, vertical beam that illuminated a thin rectangle of the wall opposite the bunks. A shadow briefly blotted out the light as a man slipped into the room, and the door closed as softly as it had opened. There was a gentle click as the catch slipped back into place, and the man's breath came fast, as though he had been running.

Brett lay very still. He could hear the intruder's hand moving over the wall close to the door; it made a soft, slithering noise, like someone smoothing out a tablecloth. He was searching for the light switch. Suddenly he found it; there was a sharp snap and the light came on.

Brett sat up. The man who had come in and switched on the light had his back turned to him, his hand still lingering on the switch. He was wearing the usual quilted jacket of the Russian deck hands, but his head was bare. His hair, cropped short into a springy mat, was the colour of sun-bleached straw. He was tall, with bulky shoulders. When he turned to face the light Brett saw that it was Peter Gubin, the Latvian.

Gubin lifted his finger in a gesture of warning, walked quickly to the port-hole, and swung the iron deadlight across it so that no light could show out and no one could peep in from the deck outside. Then he turned again to Brett.

'I 'ave come to talk to you,' he said. 'I think mebbe we 'elp each other.'

'Help each other? I don't understand.'

'Never mind. I tell you.'

Brett heard Grill stirring in the lower bunk; then Grill's hoarse voice: 'Who the devil's that? Oh, you, Pete. What you doing here at

174

this time of night?'

Gubin answered in his half-cockney, half-foreign accent: 'I 'ave to speak to both you two. It is on'y safe at night. An' not too much bloddy safe now. Lissen.'

He held up his hand and all three listened, but there was only the throb of the ship's engines to break the stillness of the night. Gubin put his ear to the door. After a moment or two he appeared satisfied.

'If Linsky asleep — okay. Sometimes I wonder, do Comrade Linsky ever take any damn sleep. Sometimes I think 'e do not 'ave to take no sleep, not at all, damn an' blast 'is bloddy eyes.'

'Why do you worry so much about Linsky?' Brett asked. 'Everybody seems scared of him. Why?'

Peter Gubin's pale blue eyes opened wide in astonishment. 'Then you not know? All this time you are in this ship, an' you not know what Comrade Linsky is?'

'I know he's a nasty piece of work. What else?'

Gubin lowered his voice to a whisper. 'My friend, I tell you. Linsky is MVD man. Secret Police. Damn an' blast swine. You unnerstan'?'

'I understand. I had half guessed as much already.' Brett was not entirely ignorant of the notorious MVD, the *Ministerstvo Vnutren-nykh Del*, or Ministry of Internal Affairs. The MVD infiltrating into factories, villages, offices, everywhere. The MVD spying, keeping constant watch, nosing out any hint of activity that might be directed against the state; having the power to spirit men away to labour camps, to prison, to Siberia, the power that Himmler's Gestapo had wielded in Nazi Germany, the power that the Cheka and the GPU had wielded before them in Russia.

So even a ship was not free from such creatures. Or was it only ships such as this, special ships, ships on important missions, that were watched over by men like Linsky?

This explained much that had been puzzling: Boyan's terror at the limping footsteps of the man; Linsky's hold over Captain Govorov himself; his presence at a meeting with so august a personage as Admiral Fedorenko. Might it not perhaps explain even more? Might it not have been Linsky who had given orders that the *Gregory Kotovsky* should flee from the scene of that collision in the Barents Sea, not pausing to search for survivors? Govorov was in command of the ship, but perhaps it was Linsky who commanded Govorov.

Brett remembered that it was Linsky who had questioned him, Linsky who had been so interested to know how he came to understand Russian, and who he was going to meet in Archangel. A man whose habit, whose duty it was to be suspicious of everyone would be suspicious even of an Englishman hauled by chance out of the fog and the sea. And he had told Linsky that he had been in Military Intelligence. To a mind such as Linsky's that could convey only one meaning — espionage. No wonder the man had been suspicious.

Gubin was looking closely into Brett's face. 'You unnerstan' now?'

'I understand.'

Gubin said: 'I tell you more 'bout Comrade Linsky. The Nazis 'ave 'im one time. They pull 'is finger off. They stretch 'is bloddy leg to make 'im talk.'

'The rack! Good God!'

'No; it is not good. If they kill 'im, that is good. But they do not kill 'im; they let 'im go. Now Linsky the man what stretch odder people's legs. Sometime mebbe 'e stretch my leg. Mebbe your leg too.'

Brett sat up very straight. An icy trickle of fear ran down his spine. Here in the small hours of the morning on board this grey Russian ship it was not easy to laugh away Gubin's words.

'They would not dare to touch us.'

Gubin smiled sadly. 'Why you think they take you to Russia? For a bloddy 'oliday per'aps?'

'They have to take us there. The ship isn't calling at any other port. When we get to Archangel we shall be able to find another ship to take us home.'

The words did not carry conviction. Brett did not even believe the truth of them himself. Gubin laughed briefly, as at some macabre joke.

'My friend, you never go 'ome, never. Russia is a big country. Russia will swallow you like you never live. Remember, you are already dead. Remember all what you 'ave seen. You think they let you come to life again? Do not be a fool. Lissen to me; I know what I talk of. I have friends in Riga one time, many friends, many relations. The bloddy Russians come; they take away my friends; they take me if I am older. Do you think my friends come back? No, they do not; they never come back, never.'

Peter Gubin paused. There were spots of fire on his high, blunt cheekbones. The bitter memory of past agonies seemed to be possessing his mind.

'They go away in cattle-trucks — fifty in a truck. It is winter; there is ice and snow. The trucks are cold, my friend, so cold. What do

178

bloddy Russians care? What do they care if a million people die of cold and starvation? Do you think they care more for two English what is already dead?'

'Why do you come here to tell us this?' Brett asked. 'Why have you come to talk to us now?'

'I come,' said Gubin, 'because I do not wish to lose my skin. I am young. I do not wish to die yet — not yet.'

'But why should you die?'

Gubin pushed his fingers through his springy mat of corn-coloured hair. He turned his head for a moment, listening. It was easy to see that he was under severe strain. The measured pulse of the engines came up from below and there were subtle creakings that one might have imagined were the voices of men whispering. Though the door was closed and the deadlight was screwed down, there was the feeling of being watched, of being overheard, of being spied upon. The evil spirit of Comrade Linsky was in the ship, and there were many others who would not hesitate to report to Linsky and do his bidding — to kill if he should order them to do so.

'I am not a Russian,' Gubin said. 'There are times when I say things it is not safe to say. It is not possible always to guard the tongue. Per'aps these things come to the long ears of Comrade Linsky. Per'aps I am on 'is list. I think so. An' I think my friends are too.'

'Your friends?'

'Josef and Nikolai. They also are Latvian. We keep together. We are not like the odders. They complain about us; they tell tales. These tales go round the ship. Then they say we are spies, an' Linsky prick up 'is ears. If we say no, we are not spies, that is not enough. Tell me 'ow you prove you are not a spy. No, we are like you; we know too much. It is not safe to know too much.'

'But surely they would not condemn you on suspicion?'

'They do not take chances. Better a dead patriot than a live saboteur. It seem to me we are all in what you call the same bloddy boat — you an' me, Josef an' Nikolai, and our big friend here. For none of us will Russia be 'ealthy.'

Grill, who had been listening to this conversation and scratching his head, suddenly interjected hoarsely and vehemently: 'You're damn right, Pete boy. But what do we do? Where's the way out? That's the question.'

'I tell you,' Gubin said. 'I tell you now. You lissen. We all go in anodder boat — a lifeboat.'

'We thought o' that. It ain't no use. You

couldn't launch it with the ship moving, and you couldn't get clear away.'

'The ship will not be moving. The ship will be sonk.'

'Sunk!' In his excitement Grill leaped out of his bunk and began to pad up and down the cabin in his bare feet, the tattoo on his chest expanding and contracting as his breath came and went. 'Sunk, by God! Now, why didn't I think of that? If the ship was sunk all the boats would have to get away. There'd be confusion. If we stuck together we could do the trick, by God we could!'

He stopped suddenly and peered into Gubin's face. 'Ah, but how do we sink the ship?'

'We blow it up. Blow it to 'ell. Bang! So.'

Grill sat down. 'Blow it up, eh? Blow it up. Well, well, well! You don't mean to do things by halves, do you?'

Brett said seriously: 'How do you propose to do that? And besides, if you blow up the ship, what about us? Do you blow us up too? There's not much future in that.'

Gubin drew up a chair and sat down also. 'Do not take me for a fool. I work things out 'ere.' He touched his forehead. 'It is all workout in 'ere, in the brain. We do not blow the ship to little bits, my friend. We blow 'oles in it — two big 'oles to let the water in.

181

Lissen; this is 'ow we do it.'

Gubin had indeed worked out the plan thoroughly. He had gone over it again and again with Josef and Nikolai. It had been in their heads for a long while, the idea of breaking for freedom, of trying to reach some country of the west where a man could live without fear. But there had to be no mistake, no chance of recapture, for that would mean death or Siberia — which were in effect one and the same.

So the Latvians had worked out their plan. An essential part of it, without which it could not be made to work, was the possession of explosives. Given the materials, they knew well how to use them. They had grown up in a hard school, during a bitter war in which sabotage was something that a young man learned as a basic lesson. Gubin had blown up a train when he was no more than twelve years old. Given the materials, they could do the job. And the materials were under their hands. They had known what they required, and they had taken it — from the *Gregory Kotovsky's* cargo. As the cargo was being discharged certain things had disappeared. Only the Latvians knew where those things had gone; only they knew where they were now hidden, waiting for the moment when they should be used to send the *Gregory*

Kotovsky to the bottom of the sea.

'You remember per'aps 'ow Josef climb the mast an' make the monkey tricks in the crow's-nest?' Gubin asked.

'I remember,' Brett said. 'We wondered why he did it.'

'We thought he was crazy,' said Grill.

'No, not so, 'e is far from crazy. It is to attract attention. When everyone look up at Josef, then Nikolai an' me, we take what we want, an' no one sees us. It is easy.'

'Good for you,' Grill said in admiration. 'You've got your heads screwed on right, I'll say that.'

Gubin went on to outline his plan. He proposed to postpone the operation until the ship was somewhere between the latitudes of twenty-five and ten degrees south, when it was reckoned that the jutting elbow of Brazil would not be more than a few hundred miles to the west. The explosion would take place at night to create the maximum amount of confusion, and allow the plotters their best chance of seizing one of the motor lifeboats of which the *Gregory Kotovsky* carried two.

'We must 'ave one of them. We do not wish to row to South America.'

To make sure that the ship should sink fairly rapidly, Gubin considered that it would be necessary to hole her both fore and aft, in number two hold and number five. The holds, containing as they did only a few tons of rock ballast, would fill rapidly, and the ballast would be extra weight pulling her down. If the operation were timed accurately, and resolutely carried out, Gubin saw no reason why it should fail.

Then all that would be necessary would be to seize a lifeboat.

'We are five strong men. We could per'aps 'ave done it with only three; but it will be easier with five. What do you think, my friends?'

Grill slapped him on the shoulder. Grill's face was creased in a grin of delight, his eyes almost vanishing behind the rolls of flesh. This was an adventure after his own heart. He would have taken part in it simply for the love of the thing, even if there had not been the incentive of saving his life.

'You're the boy, Pete. It's a great idea. Can't understand how I failed to think of it meself. Pete's the boy, ain't he, Brett? He's got brains.'

'I'm afraid there's going to be some loss of life,' Brett said soberly. 'Some of the crew may not get away.'

Gubin snapped his fingers. 'They must look out for themselves. There is odder boats. Anyway, I do not care a pin for all the odder lives. It is our lives that is of importance. Do they think of saving lives when they take my friends away in their bloddy cattle-trucks? Do they worry if a million, two million, five million die? No, they do not. Then why should we worry about a handful of their lives now? Do not tell me that you are afraid, that you will not 'elp us. Or per'aps you tell Comrade Linsky. Per'aps you rather go to Siberia.'

'Of course not,' Brett said. 'I'm with you all the way. But I hope it will not lead to loss of life.'

Gubin relaxed. It was obvious for a moment he had doubted the wisdom of letting the Englishmen into his secret.

'It need not. There is six boats. Plenty for all. But I tell you again, it do not make me to cry if all these bloddy Russians go to the bottom of the sea. It make me more to laugh very much — ha-ha — like I am mos' please. Let them rot down there in the mud. Let the fishes eat them, if the fishes will touch such filthy meat.'

'Hear, hear, Pete boy,' Grill said. 'It'd be what they call poetic justice. Didn't the bastards sink our ship? Didn't they let my shipmates drown? You want to remember that, Brett.'

'I haven't forgotten it,' Brett said. He turned to Gubin. 'When do you think we shall be in the right position to carry out this plan?'

'Two days I think it take us to be in the best place. Not tomorrow night, but the night after.'

'At what time?'

'Three-quarters way through the middle watch. At three o'clock. It must not be at the watch changing. Too many people moving then. At three o'clock Linsky will be sleeping — if he ever sleep.'

'What do you want us to do?'

'You go to the boat deck an' stand by number one boat. Get the cover off, but do not be seen. We odders will join you there. When the bang go off we lower the boat. Okay?'

Brett nodded. 'That seems clear enough. I hope all goes well.'

'It will go well if we make no mistake. We must not make mistake. Now I must go. I 'ave been 'ere too long. It is not safe I be found in 'ere.'

Gubin left the cabin as stealthily as he had entered it, switching off the light before gently opening the door. He was gone like a shadow, leaving Brett and Grill, not to sleep, but to a long whispered discussion of the plan that was, they hoped, to bring them freedom.

8

Trouble

On the morning after Gubin's nocturnal visit Brett went up to the boat deck to make an unobtrusive inspection of the boat that was intended to be their means to freedom. There were two on the starboard side and two on the port, the other two being at the after end of the ship above the poop.

The lifeboats of the *Gregory Kotovsky* were slung from modern davits that could be quickly swung outboard by means of hand-operated cranks, working on a worm and cog principle. It was a task that two reasonably strong men could accomplish in a matter of minutes; and then all that would be necessary would be to pay out the falls and allow the boat to slip gently down into the water.

That was the theory of it. In practice a heavy sea or a listing ship could upset things. It was to be hoped that when the time came the ship would not be listing too acutely, and that the sea would be smooth.

In order not to arouse any suspicion Brett

kept moving, as though he were merely taking his customary exercise on deck; but as he passed the boats he examined them keenly. They were constructed not of timber, but of metal, and canvas covers were stretched tightly over them to keep out the rain. Like the rest of the ship, they were painted a dull grey.

Number one was the for'ard of the two on the starboard side, and a propeller at one end of the keel indicated that it was, as Gubin had said, motor-driven. To Brett, the propeller seemed rather small for so large a boat, but he supposed it was big enough for the job it had to do.

'A boat like that,' Grill had said, 'will maybe do about four knots, fully loaded and in a calm sea. They're built for safety rather than speed.'

Brett hoped Gubin or one of the other Latvians knew how to work the engine. He wondered how much fuel the boat carried, and how far it could travel before the supply was exhausted. Gubin had said that in two days the ship ought to be somewhere to the east of Bahia; and, judging by the weather, which was hot and sunny, they must be already drawing near the tropics. The sea was calm, the sky feathered only with a few brilliantly white puffs of cloud. It was the right weather. Brett prayed that it would last.

'A storm could scupper us,' Grill had said. 'We got to have luck all ways. I'm keeping my fingers crossed.'

How close to the Brazilian coast would the ship pass? It might go by only a hundred miles out. The lifeboat could surely make that distance under power. On the other hand, Govorov might hold his ship farther to the east, and it might be advisable to head the lifeboat northward to Liberia or Sierra Leone. That would be a question to decide when the time came. Meanwhile, one had to concentrate on the task of getting away. It might not be easy. So many things could go wrong. The explosives . . .

Thinking deeply, Brett had stopped in his walk and was staring intently at the lifeboat, noting where the lines were fastened that held the canvas cover in place, noting the position of the crank handles which they would have to turn in order to swing the boat over the ship's side, the position also of the reels on which the falls were wound.

He started guiltily when he heard Captain Govorov's voice.

'You are interested in life-saving equipment, perhaps.'

Brett turned slowly, controlling himself. He had been a fool to stop walking, but after all no real harm had been done: an interest in lifeboats could be innocent enough. Certainly Govorov appeared to have no suspicion of any stronger motive for that interest than idle curiosity. He was quite genial. And Brett had noticed before that he was perfectly willing to exhibit any part of the ship about which there could be no point in being secretive. The ship was his pride; something very dear to his heart.

Brett said: 'I had not noticed before that these boats are made of metal. I thought the usual material was wood.'

'More usual perhaps,' Govorov answered. 'But metal is not at all uncommon. It has its advantages; it is less easily damaged and it will not burn. These boats are of a particularly modern design. Let me show you.'

He stepped towards the boat and loosened the cord securing the cover, folding the canvas back. He looked very smart, very seamanlike in his neat blue uniform and blue peaked cap. His pointed beard gave the authentic finishing touch. It occurred to Brett that Lenin, dressed in the uniform of a ship's officer, would have looked very much like Captain Govorov.

'See now; here are the buoyancy tanks along each side. The boat cannot sink even if capsized. There is the compass by that thwart; it is in gimbals, of course, and is of the latest type. Provisions are stowed in a watertight locker in the bows; water is in special tanks, and also an extra supply in those breakers that you see on the bottom boards. There is a dipper for measuring out the water. Fuel for the engine is stored aft.'

'There is some in the tank of the engine, I suppose?'

'Why yes; so that it can be started without delay.' Govorov, who had been leaning over the side of the boat, straightened himself slowly and stared at Brett. 'Why do you ask that?'

It was a slip. Brett did his best to cover it up. 'I simply thought that if the ship were sinking and you wanted to get away in a hurry you would not want to waste time in pouring fuel into the engine tank.'

'That is true. You would not, would you?' Govorov's brown eyes were curiously disconcerting. His gaze did not waver. 'If you wanted to get away in a hurry.'

He began to pull the cover back over the lifeboat and fasten it down. Only when he had made the end of the cord secure did he again address Brett. Then he said, almost gently:

'Do not, I beg you, Mr Manning, attempt

anything rash, anything foolish — for your own sake. There are many things that you can do with lifeboats, but one thing you cannot do is launch them from a ship travelling at full speed. Please remember that.'

'I did not suppose you could,' Brett said.

'I am glad to hear it.'

Govorov turned and began to walk away, but with his hand on the rail at the head of the companion-ladder he looked back and said: 'Come to my cabin this evening if you have the time to spare.' Then with a little half-salute of the right hand he disappeared down the ladder.

★ ★ ★

Brett was lying on his bunk that afternoon when Grill burst into the cabin, bringing bad news.

'We got trouble, boy; a load of trouble.'

Brett sat up. 'What's happened? Anything really serious? Anything to affect our plans?'

He had scarcely realized how deeply all his hopes were interwoven with the success of Gubin's scheme. He felt they had to get away. The atmosphere of the ship had become oppressive. It was like a prison enclosed by the stoutest of all walls — the sea. His heart sank as he heard Grill's words and saw Grill's solemn face. Trouble now could have only one meaning: something had gone wrong with the plan. Perhaps Linsky had discovered it; perhaps the explosives had been found. He had not asked Gubin where they were hidden; there was no need for him to know. Gubin and his friends would use the charges when the time came to do so.

Grill closed the door and sat down heavily. His shoulders seemed to be bowed under some load.

'Josef's been put away.'

'Put away?'

'Stowed in the cooler. Locked up. Shoved in the cells.'

'But why? What for?'

'For being a damned fool. Why couldn't he behave hisself? Why couldn't he take it just for another two days? Two days; that's all; then he'd have been free. Now he's in the cells.'

'Yes; but why? What did he do?'

'Do! He got to fighting; that's what. With one of the Russians. Pete says the man's a bastard, an informer. There's been friction there for a long time, it seems; this was just the end of it.'

'What did Josef do?'

'Slit the feller open with a knife and had a look at what made him tick. Seems like he mayn't never tick nearly so good again; in fact he might even leave off ticking altogether. But that don't help Josef none; because this boy that's been carved up is a pal of Comrade flaming Linsky, and Linsky's hopping mad. So away goes Mister Josef Slowacki to the cooler, and there he's likely to be indefinite.'

'That's bad.'

'You bet it's bad, because Pete Gubin says no Josef, no explosion, and no escape for us. He ain't going to blow holes in the ship with his pal Josef stowed away and Linsky keeping the key; because you can bet your boots Linsky ain't going to waste time letting Josef out when the ship's going down under his stinking, rotten feet.'

'Where have they shut Josef up? Do you know?'

'Oh. Yes. He's in that little deckhouse on the afterdeck, between number four and number five hatches. Seems that's what they use it for. This ship's got all the Communist fittings, including prison cells. They even have somebody on guard all the time, in spite of Linsky having the key and not letting nobody else lay hands on it. Pete says they feed the poor devil through a hatch in the door. You'd think he was a wild beast.'

'Isn't there anything we can do?'

'What can we do? Go along there and

break the place open? Nobody wouldn't take no notice, would they?' Grill stood up, and began striding angrily backward and forward in the confined space of the cabin, as though it were he who was imprisoned and not the Latvian.

'Two more days! Why couldn't he wait? Now he's upset the whole bag of tricks.'

Brett leaned his head back against the hard bulkhead behind his bunk; he felt like beating his head against it in anger, in frustration. It could not be. He would not believe that their whole plan must come to nothing because of one man's uncontrollable temper. There must surely be some way, some answer to this fresh problem. And yet, without Gubin, he and Grill were helpless; and Nikolai would follow Gubin's lead. Besides, they could no more leave Josef to perish in his cell than Gubin could, fool though Josef may have been, and angry with him though they might be.

'I must see Gubin,' Brett said. 'I've got to talk to him.'

'You'll see him,' Grill said. 'He's coming here tonight.'

★ ★ ★

Brett found Captain Govorov alone in his cabin. He was seated at his table, writing. He

195

indicated a chair with his pen, and Brett sat down.

'I will not keep you a moment. If you will allow me to finish this.'

For a while his pen moved rapidly over the paper. The creases in his forehead were deep with concentration. Perhaps he was worried also. That morning on the boat deck he had appeared more relaxed than Brett had ever known him to be. Now the care, the weariness, were in his face again.

He finished writing and put down the pen. He rested his elbows on the table and put the tips of his fingers together, forming an arch over which his velvety eyes stared at Brett.

'There has been trouble in the ship. You may perhaps have heard.'

Govorov paused. He appeared to be waiting for Brett to make some comment. Brett did not choose to do so; he did not wish to commit himself. He waited for Govorov to continue. Govorov also waited, but, seeing that Brett was going to make no reply, he went on.

'A man has been knifed. He may possibly die. That is a serious matter. The man who knifed him is Josef Slowacki. You know him?'

'I am not acquainted with the members of the crew,' Brett said.

'No?' Govorov's eyes had lost some of their

velvety quality. They had become hard. He put his hands on the table and beat a tattoo with the tips of his slender fingers.

'Slowacki is now safely locked away where he can do no more harm. He will be handed over to the appropriate authority when we get back to Russia. He is a troublemaker, and has been from the start of the voyage. There are two other troublemakers who may have to be put in safekeeping — Peter Gubin and Nikolai Vilhelms; we have had our eyes on them for some time.'

Brett stiffened. If Peter and Nikolai were locked up as well as Josef there would be the end of hope. He wondered why Govorov was telling him this. Did he have any suspicion concerning the two Englishmen? Had any rumour come to his ears that they had been having contact with the Latvians, the so-called troublemakers?

Brett noticed that behind Govorov was a door leading to an inner cabin, possibly the captain's sleeping quarters. There was a grille over the door. Could it be that Comrade Linsky was hiding in the other room? Was Govorov trying to extract some admission, some information that Linsky could seize upon?

Brett decided to move carefully.

'They are all men from the Latvian

Republic of the USSR,' Govorov continued. 'But you do not know any of them?'

'I know Gubin,' Brett said. 'I have spoken to him on various occasions.'

He knew that it would have been foolish to deny this, since it was a fact too well known throughout the ship.

'Ah yes. I believe he speaks English.'

'Very badly.'

'H'm. But you know no other members of the crew?'

'Apart from Boyan, the steward, none. Since Butler injured one of them they have not been altogether friendly.'

Captain Govorov smiled faintly. 'That is perhaps understandable.'

Brett heard a slight creak that seemed to come from the direction of the inner room. It could have been caused by the pressure of a man's shoulder on the door.

Govorov got up from his chair and his manner became more friendly. He seemed to be relieved at having put a distasteful duty behind him.

'I was going to play some more records for you, but unfortunately I have much work to do. This business of the man Josef Slowacki has upset things. You will forgive me if I ask you to go now? But first let me lend you another book — one of the classics this time.

You have read Tolstoy's *War and Peace?*'

'No, I have not.'

'Then now is your opportunity. We still have a long voyage ahead of us. You will find ample time, and I assure you you will not find it dull. Let me know what you think of Tolstoy's theory of history. You will see how he attacks the legend of Napoleon. Perhaps he is right. Who knows? Who knows the real lesson of Borodino, or the retreat from Moscow?'

He took a massive volume from his well-filled bookcase and handed it to Brett. 'A heavyweight, is it not? A combination of fact, fiction, and theory written fifty years after the event. Will such a masterpiece ever be written about the Hitlerite war of patriotism, I wonder?'

He tapped the book with his forefinger, and lowered his voice until it was hardly above a whisper. 'In here you will read how the Grande Armée, retreating over the battlefield of Borodino, was forced to pass by the corpses of men slain seven weeks earlier and still unburied. That must have been a fearful experience: to see, perhaps, the man you killed in your march forward, or the friend who was cut down at your side, to see them again in all the rottenness of decay, and wonder, for what did they die? A dream, a

199

chimera; dust and ashes. Terrible; terrible! One should never go back; never so much as look to the rear. Always on, on, wherever the path may lead. Retreat is the final bitterness, the ultimate nightmare. The bodies of the dead, the sacrificed, lie along that road, and they are a reproach to the living.'

Suddenly he thrust the book into Brett's hands. 'Go now. I have work to do.' He passed a hand over his eyes, as though feeling the weariness in them. 'So much work to do.'

Brett left the cabin, wondering, not for the first time, just what to make of Captain Govorov.

★　★　★

Peter Gubin came at two o'clock in the morning, slipping into the cabin as silently as a ghost. He closed the door and snapped on the light. The port-hole was already closed and the deadlight fastened across it. Gubin sat down on one of the chairs and stared at the two Englishmen, shaking his head sadly from side to side, the picture of despondency.

Brett had scarcely been to sleep. He had dozed fitfully, each time waking with a start and expecting to find Gubin in the cabin. But when Gubin had come he had not heard him, only waking to full consciousness as the light flooded on.

Gubin said: 'You 'ear about Josef?'

'Grill told me,' Brett said. 'Why did he do it? He's ruined everything.'

'Josef is a man what is quick-tempered. This damn Russian, 'e keep on at Josef, provoke 'im.' Gubin always referred to the other members of the crew as Russians, not accepting that nationality for himself. 'Josef can stand it no longer. Josef slice 'is big belly open — so.' Gubin demonstrated with his hand the upward thrust of the knife. 'You should 'ear 'im yell. You 'ear a pig killed? It is like that; 'e squeal bloddy murder.'

'And if he dies?'

'If 'e die, that one damn good thing. I do not weep at 'is funeral.'

'Perhaps not; but it's our funeral too — with Josef shut away.'

Gubin shrugged. He seemed resigned. 'That is 'ow things is. We can do nothing now, nothing.'

'Is there no way of getting Josef out?'

'No way without the key. Linsky 'ave that.'

'Do you know where he keeps it?'

'In his cabin, I think mos' likely. This key, it is a bloddy big key. Not damn likely 'e carry it about in 'is pocket.'

'Then we might get it from his cabin.'

201

Gubin shook his head. 'It would not be possible to go to his cabin. Linsky is a careful man, damn 'is bloddy eyes.'

'I know somebody who might be able to help us,' Brett said. 'Somebody who goes in and out of Linsky's cabin at all hours.'

'And 'oo is that?'

'Anton Boyan.'

'That steward. 'E would not do it.'

'I have a feeling he would — if we agreed to take him with us. He wants to get to America; he'd give his ears to get there. Well, here's his opportunity. What's more, he may know just where Linsky keeps his keys. He might be able to pick this one up at the right time without anyone being the wiser. I tell you Boyan is our man.'

Gubin seemed half convinced, but he was still doubtful. 'Can we trust 'im? 'E 'as no guts, that boy. Mebbe 'e tell Linsky what we do.'

'That is a risk we shall have to take. But Boyan's so keen to be a millionaire that I think he'll do anything that's likely to help him in that direction. Anyway, if he splits on us, are we any worse off? Govorov himself told me that you and Nikolai are on the black list. He was talking of locking the two of you up as well as Josef. I'm glad to see they haven't done so yet.'

'They want us to work,' Gubin said. 'They'll let us work until we get to Russia. Then they lock us up. Well, try Boyan if you like. If 'e get the key, me an' Nikolai, we do the exploding. But 'e must get the key. We do not leave Josef; you understand?'

'I understand that. I'll tackle Boyan tomorrow morning.'

'Okay.'

'I'll wring his neck if he don't agree,' Grill said. 'But he'll play.'

There was silence in the cabin for a while as each man was busy with his own thoughts. Then Gubin's head jerked up.

'Lissen!'

Brett could hear nothing but the beat of the engines and the creaking of the ship. But Gubin's ears were sharper. Keen hearing had perhaps saved his life more than once in the past. Perhaps his ear had often been cocked for the sound of the midnight knock at the door, the dreaded summons of the state police.

With a rapid, stealthy movement he was by the door, his fingers on the electric light switch. In a moment the cabin was in darkness.

Not until then did Brett also hear the sound — footsteps in the alleyway — limping footsteps. He lay back on his bunk, knowing that Linsky was moving about the ship; Linsky, never sleeping, always watchful, sniffing out trouble with his bloodhound nose.

Brett waited for the footsteps to go past. But they did not do so. They halted outside the cabin. The seconds ticked away. Brett could hear a man breathing; he wondered whether it was Gubin or Grill, or perhaps even Linsky. He waited tensely for the footsteps to sound again as the man moved away. He knew that he was listening at the door, perhaps with his ear pressed against the panels.

Then he heard the handle turning, gently, very gently. Time seemed to pass slowly. The door creaked; a line of light appeared on the bulkhead opposite Brett's bunk. He heard Grill turn over in the bunk below and give a long sigh, like a man disturbed in his sleep. Grill was acting.

A hand felt for the light switch, found it. The light suddenly flashed on and the door was pushed open. Brett sat up, blinking his eyes, as though the light had roused him from sleep.

In the doorway stood Comrade Linsky.

Brett could see Gubin, also. He was standing close up to the door on the opposite side of it from Linsky. There was no more than six inches between the two men, yet neither could see the other because the door stood between them.

In Gubin's hand was a knife; a long, pointed, sailor's sheath-knife.

Linsky stood quietly looking in, saying nothing. 'What do you want?' Brett asked.

The unshaded light was reflected in little gleams from Linsky's steel-rimmed spectacles. His cold eyes gazed bleakly from behind them. Though there had been ample opportunity to become sunburnt during the long voyage of the *Gregory Kotovsky* Linsky's face was as pallid and unhealthy in appearance as ever. He was like a man who spends all his time moving about in dark cellars; there was something slug-like about him, a creature of darkness and of slime.

Grill turned over again and yawned loudly, giving a plausible imitation of a man waking. Brett hoped he would not do anything rash. With Grill there was no telling; he might get up and bundle Linsky out of the room. Better not to resort to force — yet. Linsky was merely suspicious. It was obvious that he was not aware of Gubin's presence.

'What do you want?' Brett repeated.

Linsky pushed the door open a little wider. It almost touched Gubin.

'I thought I heard voices.'

'And what if you did? Are we not allowed to talk?'

'It is very late,' said Linsky. 'Besides, you did not wake up until I switched on the light.'

'If you did hear anything,' Brett said, 'it must have been my friend below. He talks in his sleep. It's nothing for you to worry about.'

Linsky's gaze travelled round the cabin and came to rest on the deadlight.

'It is a warm night. Why do you have the port-hole closed? Do you not like fresh air?'

'We like to sleep late. The light wakes us up.'

'How strange.'

Linsky hesitated in the doorway, his hand resting on the handle. He seemed undecided whether to come right into the cabin or to go away. Brett tried not to let his gaze stray towards Gubin, lest it should betray the seaman's presence; but out of the corner of his eye he could see Gubin's long knife gleaming.

'Tell the bastard to get to hell out of it,' Grill mumbled.

'What does your friend say?' Linsky asked.

'He says he wants to sleep, and would you mind going away?'

Linsky nodded. 'Very well. I will go. But tell him not to talk so much in his sleep. It is a bad habit, and a dangerous one. Sometimes men have suffered in health because of it. It is bad, very bad. Please remember.'

He switched the light off, closed the door, and was gone. They heard his limping step receding down the alleyway until the sound of it was swallowed in the steady beating of the ship's pulse.

Grill swore quietly. 'That was close. Too damn close.'

Brett heard Gubin's knife slide back into its sheath.

'It is close for Linsky, too. That bloddy Linsky is near one fat corpse, but 'e do not know it. Lucky for 'im 'e do not come right in.'

'Lucky for us, too,' Brett said. 'We don't want any corpses on our hands.'

'There is easy way with corpses,' Gubin said cheerfully. 'Overside, almighty damn quick. Nobody find, nobody know what 'appen. Now I wait 'ere some time, until Linsky get tired watching the door. Then I go. Okay?'

Brett did not know how long Gubin waited. In the morning when he awoke and unscrewed the deadlight only Grill was with him in the cabin. Gubin had gone as silently as he had arrived.

9

An Incident

Brett tackled Boyan when the steward brought breakfast. Boyan was a man torn between two powerful forces — fear of Linsky and desire to seize this opportunity with both hands.

But fear seemed at first to be the stronger. 'Suppose I am caught. Suppose I am caught.'

'You needn't be caught,' Brett said patiently. 'You have plenty of excuses for going to Linsky's cabin. Do you know where he keeps the key to the cells?'

'Oh, yes; I know that. He has several keys. They are on hooks above his bunk.'

'And you know which is the one we want?'

'Yes, I know. It is bigger than the others.'

'Then surely you could take it when he isn't there?'

Boyan wrung his hands, the very picture of indecision. He wished to take this step, and yet he was afraid, deeply afraid. And it was of more than Linsky that he was afraid — behind Linsky was the vast organization of the MVD.

'I could. Yes, I could. But if I should be discovered. You do not realize what they could do to me.'

'But if you are careful there is no need to be discovered. And think; just think — ' Brett seized Boyan's arm and looked into the little Armenian's black, frightened eyes. 'Think what it means to you. You will be able to go to America. You will have the chance to become a millionaire. Isn't that worth a tiny risk? You will have a big, shining car, servants to wait on you, diamond tie-pins, women. Money will buy anything, Anton; remember that. Remember the skyscrapers, Anton. Think of the dollar bills — thick wads of them, crisp and new. Think of all the Greeks, the Italians, the Germans, the Dutch, the Scandinavians — yes, and the Armenians — who have made their fortunes in the United States. Are you going to throw away your chance now just because of a little risk? I don't believe it. I don't believe you would be such a fool.'

Brett could see that Boyan was wavering; he pressed home his argument.

'It is such a little thing to do. And the risk is so small. Just this one little thing and then — freedom. We cannot fail, I tell you. We will get to Brazil; from there to the United States.'

'But if I got there, would they let me stay? Perhaps they would say, no, you must go back to Russia, where you came from. That is where you belong.'

'They would not do so; I promise you. You will ask for political asylum and they will grant it; they are bound to. Then you get a job; you become an American citizen; you make money; you become rich as Rockefeller.'

Boyan could hold out no longer. Avarice had overcome fear.

'I will do it. If I die for it, I will do it.'

Brett slapped him on the shoulder. 'Good man. Tonight, then, you will get the key and bring it to me here. Do not come too early, but do not be later than half-past two. You understand?'

'Yes, I understand. I will do it.'

Brett put a hand on each of Boyan's shoulders and looked him straight in the eyes.

'And do not betray us. If you betray us I shall be obliged to tell Comrade Linsky all that you have told me about yourself. He might be interested to learn that you wish to escape from Russia and run away to America.'

Boyan's eyes dilated with terror. He tugged at Brett's sleeve.

'You will not tell! You will not tell! You promised me you would not tell!'

'And I will not — if you are straight with

us. I was simply warning you. Do not try any tricks or it may be the worse for you.'

'I will not betray you. I swear it.'

'All right, then. Now you'd better go. You've been here too long already. Linsky is suspicious enough as it is. We don't want to give him any cause to be more so. I think he knows something is in the wind, but I feel certain he doesn't know what it is. Before long he will find out, but the knowledge will not please him one little bit. Go on. Be off with you.'

Boyan went, trembling with the twin emotions of hope and terror.

Grill, who had all this while been lying on his bunk, got up and yawned.

'Well? Is he going to do it? He looked scared out of his ruddy wits.'

'He was scared, but he'll do it.'

'You don't think he'll blow the gaff? He don't appear to me to be remarkable for guts.'

'I threatened to tell Linsky about his little ideas if he let us down. He won't risk that. Besides, he's keen to be a millionaire, and this'll be a step on the right road.'

Grill laughed. 'If that's what he's going to be we'd better keep in touch. We might be able to sting him for a few dollars one day.'

'That's true. It might be handy to have a rich friend in the States.'

After breakfast Brett went down to the afterdeck to have a look at the deckhouse in which Josef was imprisoned. It would be dark when they went to release him, and it would be advisable to have the layout firmly fixed in the mind beforehand.

The timing would have to be accurate. Josef must not be released too soon, in case the alarm should be given and spread through the ship. The plan was for Brett and Grill to deal with the matter of Josef's escape while Peter and Nikolai were setting the charges in the holds. The Latvians would have to go down through the inspection hatches, and it was fortunate that there would be no moon to reveal their activities to the officer of the watch or anyone else who might be awake. It was to be hoped that Linsky would be asleep, but that was something that could not be relied upon.

The deckhouse was a small rectangular structure built at the foot of the mainmast, between the hatches of number four and number five holds. It had a door opening outward on the port side, and this was hooked back against the wooden wall of the house to let in light and air. There were no windows.

Glancing in as he passed, Brett could see that there was a passage-way running the whole length of the house, possibly four or five feet wide. On the right of this passage were two other doors — obviously those of the cells, in one of which Josef was a prisoner.

A seaman was sitting on a box at the far end of the passage, leaning back against the wall, apparently half asleep. It was a warm and drowsy day, and the sea was calm and smooth as a great bowl of pale blue dye.

Brett went on past the deckhouse as far as the poop, turned and walked back. Two seamen passed him, scarcely troubling to turn their heads, and Brett did not address them. He wondered what they thought about Josef, whether they were bitter against him for what he had done, or whether, in the secrecy of their hearts, some of them sympathized with the Latvian. It would be impossible to tell.

Brett climbed the ladder amidships, thinking of what was so soon to happen, so soon to throw the ship into confusion if all went according to plan. He wondered how powerful the explosive charges were, and how much damage they would do to the ship. Gubin had assured him that he knew all about that part of the business; but could anybody be quite sure just exactly how a charge of high explosive would act?

Well, that was not for him to worry about. He had his own task: to take the key from

Boyan and help Grill to release Josef. They would have to silence the guard. Then there would be the boat to make sure of. There might well be a struggle; in fact it was almost certain that there would be a struggle to keep others from getting into that particular boat. They would have to act quickly and ruthlessly. Perhaps he ought to look about for a weapon.

At the top of the ladder he came face to face with Linsky. Linsky looked tired. Probably he had not had much sleep. That was all to the good: he might be inclined to sleep all the more soundly this coming night.

'A pleasant day,' Brett observed.

Linsky did not appear to be interested in the weather. He seemed to be in a bad temper; and when Linsky was in a bad temper his voice became more squeaky than ever, reaching up to a high, brittle note.

'Why have you been down to that deck?'

Brett answered with studied innocence. 'I have been taking exercise. I should not care to become fat.'

Linsky made a little gesture of impatience. Brett wondered whether he had taken the remark to be an oblique reference to his own rather plump figure. Perhaps there was a chink there in his armour. Even a man as unattractive as Linsky might have his quota of vanity.

'In future,' Linsky said, 'please remain on the upper deck.'

'Is that an order?'

'If you wish. Yes.'

'Whose order — yours or Captain Govorov's?'

'It does not matter whose order it is. You will please to obey. You would not, I suppose, wish to have your liberty even more strictly curtailed.'

Linsky's voice was completely expressionless now. He had rigid command of himself. But the threat was unmistakable. It would be foolish to anger the man at this stage, though Brett resented being told by such a creature just what he might and might not do.

Brett had often tried to understand Linsky's mentality, but without much success. The man had suffered; the lack of a finger, the limp — these bore witness to the fact; and suffering could bring out the worst as well as the best in a man. Linsky had endured torture, yet perhaps he had not despised his torturers, perhaps had not even hated them, more than he hated all mankind; perhaps he had simply envied them their power to inflict pain. It might have been the ambition one day to wield a similar power that had given him the strength to endure and to live. He looked a sadist; he was no doubt cunning in his narrow way; but his mind was essentially a small mind, unaffected by broad issues. He could be none the less dangerous for that.

'You understand?'

'Perfectly. In future I will take my exercise up here.' Brett walked past Linsky and went to his cabin. He did not know how long he could control himself in the pallid comrade's presence; and the less he said to Linsky, the less likely was he to let fall any hint of what was afoot. Linsky would not need a very broad hint.

Captain Govorov sent another invitation for Brett to visit him in his cabin that evening. Grill was suspicious. 'What's he want to see you for? D'you think he's got wind of what's coming off tonight?'

Brett shook his head. 'I don't see how he could.'

'Unless that little devil, Boyan, has split.'

'I don't think he has. I think we can rely on him. You can usually rely on a man when you've got a hold over him, and we've certainly got a hold over our little friend.'

'Will you go?'

Grill was busy sharpening his sheath-knife on a strip of emery cloth that he had found in one of his many pockets. The knife had a stout blade and a wicked-looking point, almost like a dagger. Grill did not say why he was sharpening it, but Brett guessed that he believed the time might not be far distant when he would have need of it. Brett hoped the knife would not be needed, but he knew Grill well enough to realize that he would not hesitate to use it — preferably on Comrade Linsky.

'Yes; I shall go. He might think it strange if I didn't. You can't very well plead a previous engagement in circumstances like these.'

'Okay; but watch your step. We don't want anything else to go wrong.'

'Nothing will go wrong. Don't worry.'

'I ain't worrying. I'm just being careful.'

Govorov had the gramophone already out when Brett arrived.

'Tonight,' he said, 'I will play you the records which it was not possible to play last night. But first a glass of vodka, eh?'

Brett accepted the vodka and one of Govorov's cardboard-tipped cigarettes.

'Tonight,' Govorov said, 'no opera. I am in another mood. The polite host would consult the wishes of his guest. I ask you to bear with me this one night, only this one night. I promise you I will not again inflict my own choice upon you.'

Govorov's record library seemed to be as

wide and varied as his library of books. He played recordings of Menuhin, Kreisler, Oistrakh, Casals, Horowitz, and many others; and all the while, when he was not manipulating the machine, he sat back in his chair with eyes closed, listening to the music. His face had a greyish tinge, and he looked utterly weary. There were dark pouches under his eyes, as though he had not slept for weeks. Sometimes a nerve would quiver in his cheek.

Only at the last did he come back to the human voice. Then it was his favourite — Chaliapin; and the song was Tchaikovsky's *None But the Lonely Heart*. The song, with its great burden of lament and sadness, seemed to strike deep into Govorov's own heart; it seemed to match his mood completely. When he put the gramophone away there were tears in his eyes which he scarcely attempted to conceal.

He began to pace up and down the room in silence, his head bowed. Then suddenly he stopped moving, sat down again in his chair, and began to talk. In his deep, musical voice he told of his boyhood in Russia before the revolution of 1917; and Brett, listening to that voice, wondered what it was that had released this flood of memories.

'My father,' Govorov said, 'was a doctor in a country district. He had a small estate some hundred kilometres to the west of Moscow. He was a good man, and the peasants loved him; he was not only their doctor, attending them in every sickness, at birth, and at death, in winter as in summer, but he was also their friend, their adviser, the one to whom they brought all their problems. I think he settled more disputes among them than ever were settled in the courts of law. They called him the Little Physician, for he was a very small man, though so full of strength and energy. I never knew my mother; she died when I was born . . .'

Brett sat in his chair, watching Govorov, watching the play of emotion in the man's features as he told of those days, long since vanished into oblivion. He wondered how often Govorov had spoken of these things; he wondered whether he had ever spoken of them before; and he wondered why Govorov should have chosen him to be the recipient of his memories.

Govorov spoke quietly, even sadly, but there was a spellbinding quality about his description of life in Russia forty years ago. He told of long journeys in troikas, in summer, when the great fields of corn were undulating in the wind like an endless golden sea; of winter sleigh journeys, with the frozen snow hissing under the runners and the bells jingling on the horses; of the dismal howling of wolves in the bleak forests; of Christmas festivities and the lighted trees; of the vast plains of Russia sweeping away to the horizon, and the small villages, with their clusters of log houses and their little wooden churches. It all came out in a great tide of words like a nostalgic memory that a man has kept dammed up too long, because it can be told to no one.

Then it was over; the tale was finished. This time Brett did not look to the door behind Govorov's chair. He knew that this time Linsky was not waiting in the inner room and listening, for these words had not been for Linsky's ears.

For a while Govorov sat silent, and Brett did not break that silence. Then Govorov said:

'Tomorrow there will be a funeral — a sea burial. The man Tolbukhin, the man that Josef Slowacki stabbed, is dead.'

He put a hand over his face and muttered, as though to himself: 'The same, always the same from beginning to end. Blood, blood, blood; always blood; more and more and more. Is this the way? Is this truly the way?'

After a moment he looked up and said: 'I must ask you to leave me now. I have much to do — matters to arrange. All must be in order. No loose ends.'

Then he stood up and held out his hand. 'I am glad to have talked with you,' he said. 'Very glad. I hope that in spite of everything you will always keep not too bad an opinion of me.'

Brett shook Govorov's hand in some bewilderment. The Russian had spoken almost as though this were to be their last meeting. Then, just as Brett was leaving the room, he said: 'Tell Linsky — ' He paused and his forehead creased, as though he were thinking hard what to say; but after a moment he gave a little nervous flutter of the right hand, and said abruptly: 'No; nothing, nothing. Leave me.'

★ ★ ★

It was ten o'clock when the news ran through the ship like flame — that Captain Govorov had shot himself through the head with an automatic pistol, and was lying dead in his cabin.

Boyan carried the news to Brett, Boyan shaking with fear and anxiety.

'What do we do now? What do we do now?'

Brett could scarcely believe that it was true. So short a time before Govorov had been playing records and talking to him. And yet, when he came to think of it, he remembered the strangeness in Govorov's manner and that final handshake. It had been the handshake of a man taking leave of life.

Brett found it profoundly moving that it should have been with him, a foreigner, that Govorov had chosen to spend the last few hours of his life, that to him Govorov should have recounted his memories for that last, and perhaps only, time.

And then this strange, lonely man had set his affairs in order and had taken up the gun that was to end it all.

But it was no use thinking of that. Govorov was dead and the question was, how would his death affect their plans? The ship would be in a ferment. Would that ferment die down in time? It was necessary to speak to Gubin, but it was not safe to go to the Latvian. They must walk now with the circumspection of men treading through a minefield. The situation was explosive in more senses than one.

Boyan pulled at his arm. 'What do we do?'

'Carry on with the plan,' Brett said. 'You must get the key tonight.'

'But if I am discovered. If Linsky catches me — ' Boyan was trembling in an agony of indecision. What little spirit he had seemed all to have been knocked out of him by this shock.

'There is no more reason why he should catch you now than there was before. Less in fact. Comrade Linsky is going to be busy, I think. You've got to do it. There is no question of drawing back now. We are committed.'

Boyan went away shaking his head, his face pale. But he had promised that he would do his part, and with that promise Brett had to be content. Boyan was a weak peg for the entire enterprise to hang upon, but they could not do without him. It was to be hoped that his great desire to reach America would overcome his fears.

Ten minutes after Boyan had left the third officer came, with a request that Brett should go to Captain Govorov's cabin. Comrade Linsky desired to speak with him there.

Brett found Linsky seated in Govorov's chair at Govorov's table, as though he had now taken over without disguise that command which he had always exercised in the background. The body of the captain had been carried into the inner room, but the weapon which he had used to rid himself of a life he could no longer endure lay on the table in front of Linsky. Brett found his eyes drawn irresistibly to its black and deadly shape as to some gruesome sight.

Linsky looked even more tired than he had

done earlier in the day. It was very hot in the cabin and there were little drops of sweat on his forehead and upper lip. Even the sweat seemed to be pallid and unhealthy, like the evil moisture that drips from the walls of old dungeons.

But Linsky was wide awake; the tiredness had not spread to his eyes. Somehow, Brett found it difficult to imagine Linsky with his eyes closed; they were always watchful; cold and watchful as the eyes of a snake. One might have imagined that the very lids had been cut away so that they should not betray him into missing a single move.

'Captain Govorov is dead,' said Linsky, in his squeaky voice.

'So I have heard.'

Linsky put his hands on the table, spreading out the fingers so that the gap in the left hand was much in evidence. He did not take his cold, passionless eyes from Brett's face.

'I believe that you were the last to see him alive. Is that so?'

'I don't know,' Brett answered. 'I was with him until about nine o'clock.'

'What did you do then?'

'I went to my cabin.'

It occurred suddenly to Brett that perhaps Linsky believed he had shot Govorov, but

Linsky's next words relieved his anxiety on that point.

'And at ten o'clock Captain Govorov shot himself.' Linsky was regarding Brett keenly; his eyes never wavered. There was something oddly disquieting about that steady, penetrating stare; it seemed to be accentuated rather than softened by the wide, steel-rimmed glasses, as though they were lenses expressly provided for the purpose of concentrating the strength of it, of pin-pointing it on the spot at which it was directed.

'You appear to be relieved,' Linsky said. He seemed to have read Brett's thoughts. 'No; I do not suspect you of killing him. It is perhaps fortunate for you that I was near this cabin when the shot was fired. I came in immediately and found him. He was sitting in this chair.'

It appeared to give Linsky a certain gruesome pleasure to be sitting in the very chair in which Captain Govorov had shot himself not more than half an hour earlier.

'Then what do you wish to question me about?' Brett asked.

'You were the last to see him alive,' Linsky repeated. 'I understand that you were with him for some time this evening. I want you to tell me exactly how Captain Govorov behaved, and what he said to you.'

'He did not tell me he was going to shoot himself, if that is what you mean.'

Linsky permitted himself a slight twitch of the upper lip, which might have been a grimace of impatience. He took his hands off the table, folded them over his stomach and leaned back in his chair.

'I had not imagined that he did. It is not the usual practice of suicides to inform anyone of their intentions.' Linsky gave the impression that he had had considerable experience in such matters. 'Nevertheless, his actions, his conversation, may provide some clue to his reasons. Please describe to me exactly what they were.'

'Very well,' Brett said; 'I will tell you. First he played a number of gramophone records. The last one was *None But the Lonely Heart*, if that's any help to you.'

Linsky fluttered the fingers on his maimed left hand. 'Go on; go on. After he had finished playing records, what then?'

'Then he began to talk about his boyhood. He told me of his father, who was a doctor.'

Linsky nodded. Brett suspected that he knew all about Govorov's origins, had it all down in some dossier.

'He spoke about the days before the 1917 revolution. There was nothing important just a man recalling his youth.'

226

'Did he say that those days were better than the present?'

'No.'

'But he gave that impression, perhaps?'

'I don't know that he did. It never occurred to me.'

'And after that?'

'Then he told me that there would be a sea-burial tomorrow.'

Linsky's head jerked up. 'He said that?'

'Yes. Because the seaman, Tolbukhin, was dead.'

'Oh; because of that. Yes, of course; the man who was stabbed.'

'And after that he said he had work to do, affairs to put in order; and I left him. Before I went he shook hands, and said he hoped I would always keep a good opinion of him — in spite of everything.'

'That was all?'

'Yes.'

Linsky was silent for a time. He seemed to be puzzled. Brett guessed that here was something that could not be satisfactorily explained by his narrow mind. Perhaps it would not occur to a man of Linsky's character that anyone could become so weary of the kind of life he was forced to lead, the acts he was forced to commit in the name of duty, that at last the burden should be too

227

heavy to bear. Govorov was a man who might at one time have had visions, but those visions had been swept away; and he had seen the shoddiness that lay behind. Deprived of his visions, he had no longer any desire to live.

But if Linsky could not think all that out for himself Brett was not going to suggest it to him. Let Linsky remain puzzled.

One thing was fortunate — that he had been near at hand when the shot was fired. If there had been any suspicion of murder there was no telling what might have happened. Arrests might have been made, and who more likely to be arrested than he or Grill or the Latvians? It was essential that for a few more hours at least they should retain their liberty.

At last Linsky said: 'Very well. That is all.'

It was a dismissal. Brett went back to his cabin and found Grill much relieved to see him.

'Thought they might have nabbed you, boy. I'd have killed that Linsky if they had.'

'You may get the chance yet,' Brett said. 'Meanwhile we've just got to wait, and hope that somebody goes to sleep in this damned ship before three o'clock.'

10

Dead of Night

Brett envied Grill his capacity to sleep whatever the circumstances.

'We've got plenty to do later on,' Grill had said. 'So I'm going to do some blanket drill, while I've got the chance.'

Brett also lay on his bunk, but he did not sleep. He lay awake and listening — listening to the calm, steady breathing of Grill in the bunk below, to the ticking of his wrist-watch, which every now and then he would press to his ear, to the noises of the ship, to the sound of feet passing up and down the alleyway. At first the sound of footsteps had been frequent, men hurrying back and forth, as though the death of the captain had been like some disaster in an ant-heap that sends the ants scurrying here and there, apparently without object, experiencing only the panic that comes when the set order of affairs is disturbed.

But as the hours passed the sounds gradually died away. Sleep, even in this emergency, had claimed its due.

At two o'clock Gubin slipped into the cabin to whisper that all was set.

'You 'ave the key?'

'Not yet,' Brett said. 'Boyan has another half-hour.'

'That damn steward, 'e better not fail,' Gubin said, and went away.

The ship was perfectly steady, moving on into the night with scarcely the suggestion of a roll. With only the ballast of water and rock at the bottom of the holds to keep her down, she was inclined to roll at the slightest provocation. It was obvious, therefore, that the sea was completely placid; and for this Brett was thankful. A storm now would have upset all their calculations.

The luminous hands of his watch crawled down to half-past two, and still Boyan had not come. Grill awoke, having the ability not only to sleep at will, but to awake at a given time. He got up, switched the light on, and thrust his feet into a pair of the rope sandals that he had made. He had not undressed and was still in the blue cotton shirt and trousers that Govorov had provided out of the ship's stores. He pulled a jersey and jacket over the shirt. Though it was stiflingly hot in the cabin it might not be so hot in the boat. On his cannon-ball head he put a knitted cap.

'That Boyan been yet?'

'No,' Brett said. 'I'm getting worried. He ought to have been here by now.'

Brett also put his feet into a pair of Grill's rope sandals. You could move silently, treading on rope; it did not ring on iron as leather did. He looked at his watch again. It was twenty-five to three. Gubin and Nikolai would be down in the holds fixing the charges. And still Boyan had not come. Time was running out.

Grill was rubbing the stubble on his chin. He began to pull at his lower lip, allowing it to flip back with a plopping sound. That and the beating of the ship's engines were the only noises in the cabin.

'Twenty to three,' Brett said. 'We can't wait much longer. It'll soon be zero hour for the fireworks.'

He wondered whether Boyan had fallen foul of Linsky, or whether his nerve had failed him at the last moment. They should never have trusted so poor a tool. They should have known better. And now it was too late.

The door-handle turned and Boyan slipped in, sweat coursing down his face. He held out a trembling hand with a key in it.

'There it is. I got it. I had to wait for Linsky to be out of the way. He is not in his cabin. He is about the ship somewhere. You will have to be careful.'

'Right,' Brett said. 'Now go to the boat deck. Start loosening the cover on number one lifeboat. But for God's sake, don't be seen.'

He put the key in his pocket and moved to the door. He opened it an inch or two, then closed it hurriedly. A man was coming down the alleyway. They could hear him humming a Russian folksong, and they waited, sweating, in the hot cabin, waiting for the man to pass.

The sound of the footsteps ceased outside the door; then the humming stopped also and they heard the scrape of a match. The man was obviously lighting a cigarette or a pipe. He seemed in no hurry to move on, perhaps getting the pipe burning to his satisfaction. They could smell the strong tobacco. Precious seconds ticked away, each one like an hour. Would the man never go?

He moved away at last and the sound of his footsteps gradually faded.

'Now,' Brett said. He switched off the light, opened the door, and looked out. The alleyway was deserted.

'Come on!'

They moved rapidly and silently down the alleyway, past the doors of other cabins, many of which were hooked open because of the heat. They could hear men snoring. From one cabin a voice mumbled something; but they did not answer and they did not stop. Then they were out in the open with the fresh night air on their faces.

Boyan disappeared silently, making for the boat deck. Brett and Grill moved to the left, feeling along the rails for the ladder that led down to the afterdeck. It was a starry, moonless night, in which objects would be faintly visible when their eyes became accustomed to the dark. But they knew the way from memory, almost by instinct. In a moment they were down the ladder and moving along the afterdeck, their feet silent on the iron. Grill stubbed his toe against some hard metal obstacle and swore softly and briefly.

Then they saw the dark mass of the deckhouse looming up in front of them.

'We're here,' Brett whispered.

They were on the opposite side from the door. They could see a beam of light shining out from the opening and illuminating a stretch of the port bulwarks. It would be hot in the deckhouse, and obviously the guard had left the door open for ventilation.

Grill and Brett pressed themselves against the deckhouse, squeezing between it and the coaming of number four hatch. Stepping over the steam-pipes that ran fore and aft along the deck, they came to the corner of the

233

deckhouse, and Brett peered cautiously into the doorway.

The guard was seated on his box at the far end of the short passage, with his head lolling on his chest. He appeared to be dozing.

'I'll get him,' Grill whispered.

He moved swiftly and silently, and the guard, a small, grey-haired man, woke to his danger too late. He half rose from the box before Grill struck him with a short piece of flat iron bar like a tyre-lever, that Brett had not known he possessed.

The man slumped forward and lay on the floor, his grey hair stained with a trickle of dark blood.

'Shut the door,' Grill said.

Brett unhooked the door of the deckhouse and drew it shut. He heard Josef's voice coming from one of the cells.

'Who is that? What is happening?'

'Keep quiet,' Brett said. 'We are going to let you out.'

The cell door was of iron, with a barred window, which could be slid to one side so that food could be passed to the prisoner without opening the door. Brett saw Josef's gaunt face with its two days' growth of beard framed in the window.

'We have less than fifteen minutes before the ship blows up. Peter and Nikolai are fixing the charges.'

He took the key from his pocket and inserted it in the lock of the door. He turned it. The key moved a little way and then stopped. He put more pressure on it, but it would go no farther. He tried twisting it back again; he rattled it up and down; but all without effect.

Josef stared at him through the barred window, an expression of growing anxiety on his thin face.

'You let me out, please. You let me out.'

'Here,' Grill said impatiently. 'Let me have a go.' He took hold of the key with his massive hand and twisted it, exerting all the pressure of which he was capable. Suddenly the key gave way under his grip and he found himself staring foolishly at the useless, broken end.

'The damned rotten tool!'

The key was broken, one part of it jammed irretrievably in the lock, and the door as firmly secured as ever.

'What in hell do we do now?'

Josef's voice came from inside the cell, urgent, anxious, a little fearful.

'You hurry, please. You let me out before we blow up.'

'The key is broken in halves,' Brett said. 'We can't move the lock.'

Josef gave a cry of dismay. 'Do not leave me in here. You must let me out. Do not leave me here when the ship sinks.'

'We will not do that,' Brett said. But it was easier to assure Josef that they would not leave him than it was to see how they were going to get him out of his prison.

Both Brett and Grill swung round in alarm as the door of the deckhouse opened. But it was Gubin who slipped in.

'You 'urry,' Gubin said urgently. 'What you waiting for? Ten minutes; then the bloddy bang.'

Grill showed him the end of the key. 'It broke off. Now we can't open the flaming door.'

'You'll have to go back and stop the charge,' Brett said. 'If not, Josef's for the high jump.'

Gubin shook his head vehemently. 'Not possible now.' He pointed down at the deck. 'Right onder 'ere, it is. Right onder our bloddy big feet.'

The grey-haired guard stirred and groaned, as though his mind were struggling to find its way back to consciousness; but he did not wake. Gubin glanced down at him and pushed him aside contemptuously with his foot.

Josef peered through the barred window of

236

his cell, seeing new hope in the presence of his friend.

'Peter, you get me out of here. You do it, Peter. You hurry, hurry.' His voice rose hysterically.

Gubin snarled back at him in Russian. 'Stop that noise. You want the whole crew waked up?'

Grill had been examining the lock. Now he looked up.

'There's a gap here, see, between the door and the jamb. You can see the tongue of the lock. You must have got it back part way, Brett; it's only catching by a wee bit. Maybe we could lever it open.'

He picked up the iron bar with which he had hit the guard and eased it into the gap.

'Now then, you two; give me a hand.'

The bar was no more than a foot and a half long and did not provide a great deal of leverage, but all three put their weight on it and heaved. The door groaned, but did not move.

'One more try. Give it all you got this time.'

They put every ounce of their weight on the bar and suddenly found themselves lying on the floor in a tumbled heap. With a grinding screech the tongue of the lock had torn away the rusty edge of the socket in which it had been caught and the door was open.

They scrambled to their feet as Josef came bounding out of his prison.

'Quick,' Gubin cried. 'Not many minutes left now.'

He seized Josef's arm and hurried him out of the deckhouse. Grill was about to follow when Brett stopped him. He pointed to the guard, still lying senseless on the floor.

'What about him? We can't leave him there to be blown up or drowned.'

'Why not?' Grill said. 'Best thing for him. He won't be no more trouble then.'

'No; we can't do it. We've got to give the poor devil a chance.'

Grill shrugged his shoulders. 'Okay, okay; if that's the way you feel about it I'll carry the little runt.'

He stooped down and picking up the Russian as though he had been a child, slung him across his shoulder.

'Get weaving, then.'

When they came out of the deckhouse Gubin and Josef had already disappeared in the direction of the boat deck. Grill, staggering a little under his burden, groped forward into the darkness, and Brett followed, expecting at any moment to hear the rumble of the explosion in number four hold. There could not be many seconds left now.

When they came to the ladder amidships

there was no sign of the Latvians. Gubin was not the man to waste precious time; probably he and Josef were already with Boyan at work on the lifeboat, getting it ready for imminent launching.

The ship was silent, pressing blindly on into the warm and silent night, like a man who strides confidently forward, unaware that the poison that shall so shortly kill him is already planted within his body. But perhaps, after all, the ship was not wholly unaware of danger; perhaps the slight, scarcely perceptible vibration running through it was in fact a shiver of apprehension.

Above the masts the stars glittered in summer brilliance, splattered upon the sky like splashings of gold paint from a decorator's brush. From somewhere came a sound like a deep hollow clanging, as though someone were beating an iron tank with a sledge-hammer. Then, as suddenly as it had begun, the clanging ceased.

Grill went up the ladder, panting under his load, and Brett followed. As they reached the higher deck Brett saw Linsky and knew that they were in for trouble.

Linsky came out of a doorway in the midships accommodation, and the light from the doorway shone out in a wide beam, revealing the heavy figure of Grill with his burden.

Brett saw Linsky's hand come slowly up and there was a short-barrelled revolver in the hand. Linsky's voice, high and squeaking, broke the silence.

'Stop where you are. If you move I will shoot.'

Grill stopped. He could not have understood the words, but the menace and meaning of the revolver would have been apparent to any but a blind man. Linsky moved forward a pace or two.

'What are you doing? Why are you not in your cabin?'

It was Brett who answered. 'Playing a game, perhaps. Would you like to join in?'

For an instant Linsky's gaze shifted from Grill, searching the shadow in which Brett was standing. It was obvious that until then he had not been aware that he had more than one to deal with.

The momentary loss of vigilance was his undoing. Grill seized the opportunity without hesitation. He lunged suddenly forward, and with a heave of his great shoulder, like a man tossing a caber, he sent the unconscious guard flying straight at Linsky.

Linsky's gun spurted red flame, but the bullet embedded itself in the unfortunate human missile. Then the body struck him full in the chest, and flung him back through the doorway. He fell with the body on top of him.

At that moment the deck seemed to leap and shudder under Brett's feet. He staggered against the rails, and the great roar of the explosion burst in his ears, flailing the eardrums with its tempest blows.

Looking back towards the stern of the ship, he saw a red gush of fire blasted up into the night. The deckhouse, in which only a few minutes earlier they had been struggling to effect Josef's release, seemed to burst open like a paper bag, and the deck vomited like the crater of a volcano.

Gubin had most certainly underestimated the strength of his explosive charge. This must have torn a hole in the side of the ship big enough for a river to flow through.

Grill pulled at Brett's sleeve. 'Come on, boy. No time to waste. Up to the boat deck.'

They found the boat deck ladder and clambered up it. 'Come on; come on. Hurry!'

Brett needed no urging, but fast though they moved, they had not reached the boat when Nikolai's charge exploded for'ard with possibly even greater effect than the one in the after hold. The vessel shuddered as if she had struck a rock at full speed, and a fountain of flame and debris shot high in the air.

The bridge was suddenly silhouetted against the crimson glare of the explosion, and Brett saw the figure of a man go down as though he had been shot. Staggered by the shock, he clutched at a stanchion to prevent himself from falling, but Grill seized his arm again, and there was no mistaking the note of urgency in Grill's hoarse voice.

'Come on, boy. By God, she'll go down like a ruddy stone. Come on.'

The ship had taken a list to port and the list was slowly but steadily increasing. Brett could feel the deck tilting under his feet as he followed Grill to number one boat station. Men were at work on the davits, dark shadows against the skyline.

Gubin's anxious voice cried out. 'Who is that?'

'All right,' Brett said. 'We had trouble with Linsky.'

Gubin did not pause to ask what form the trouble had taken. He turned again to the job in hand.

Lights suddenly flashed on, revealing Boyan and the three Latvians. Then, as suddenly as they had appeared, the lights faded out and the whole ship was in darkness, except for the red glow of flames beyond the high wall of the bridge. The explosion in the forward hold had started a fire and the stench of burning paint and timber came wafting back to them, the smoke stinging their eyes and nostrils.

The ship was still moving forward, but she was no longer doing so under power. The engines had been stopped and the momentum was gradually failing. She was holed fore and aft, and the water flooding into her holds was taking the way off her like brakes applied to a car.

The cover was off the lifeboat and the cranks of the davits were grinding harshly. The boat began to swing up and out. But it was never to be launched, for suddenly the ship took a deeper list to port and the boat came lunging heavily inboard as the deck tilted at an acute angle.

Brett heard Boyan yell out in pain as the boat struck him. Then Brett, too, was thrown off his feet. The deck seemed to come up and hit him; he rolled over and over before coming to a halt with something hard and immovable ramming him in the back.

He could smell the odour of hot oil breathing over him, and when he had struggled up he saw that what had stopped him was the engine-room skylight, its glass shutters propped open for ventilation.

Everything had become confused. There was a sound of shouting and cursing, cries of terror and dismay; men were running here and there, some with torches spraying narrow beams of light over the deck and superstructure; a hissing, roaring gush of steam was issuing from the funnel and falling like drops of rain; the deck was sloping to port at an angle of thirty degrees; and over all was the lurid glow of the fire burning in the for'ard part of the ship. It was like a scene from Dante's *Inferno*.

As Brett, still dazed by his fall, stood balancing himself against the slope of the deck, he heard Grill shouting.

'Brett, where are you? Where are you, boy?'

He yelled back: 'Here I am, Grill; over here.'

Grill loomed up in front of him. 'We got to take one of the port boats now. We can't launch these on this side. We got to keep together.'

They groped and slithered down to the port rails, and it was like moving down the roof of a house. Here they found more confusion; men seemed to have gone crazy with terror.

'Bastards,' Grill said. 'Silly bastards!'

The for'ard of the two boats on this side, the one with the motor, was already swinging outboard, and the falls were just being released. An officer with an electric torch in his hand was yelling orders, trying to make himself heard above the din.

'Look,' Grill said. 'Look in the boat.'

The torch beam had come to rest momentarily on the plump, squat figure of Linsky, sitting in the sternsheets as the boat was lowered. Linsky was taking no chances; the revolver was gripped in his right hand, and he was watchful. The torchlight glimmered on his spectacles and showed his pale face and close-cropped head. Then it flickered away.

'That boat's no good,' Grill said. 'We'll have to take the other.'

A man bumped into Brett as he came slithering down the deck. It was Gubin.

'You two come quick, quick.'

Brett grabbed Gubin's arm, yelling in his ear. 'Linsky is in the for'ard boat.'

'Then we take the odder.'

Nobody appeared to be paying any attention to correct boat stations. Everyone was crowding to the motor lifeboat, which was obviously the one that was getting away first. Some were already in it; some slithered down the life-lines as it was lowered.

'Anton, Nikolai, Josef!' Gubin bellowed. 'Here!' Miraculously, three figures appeared out of the gloom and began to work on the second lifeboat, ripping the cover off, feverishly turning the cranks, letting go the falls; Gubin barking out orders.

Brett could never remember clearly how the boat was launched. He remembered only that as it went down towards the sea the sea came up to meet it. He remembered water lapping over the boat deck. He remembered wrestling to release one end of the lifeboat from its hook and casting loose the painter. And he remembered wondering, in a strangely detached way, whether they would get clear before the ship's funnel came down like a falling chimney and thrust them under.

Even when they were afloat on a calm, dark sea with nothing visible but the shadowy survivors in the boat, and all around them the black velvet of the night, he could not be clear in his mind just how it had happened.

They were all there — Boyan, Gubin, Slowacki, Vilhelms, Grill, and himself. It had not gone according to plan. There was no motor in the lifeboat; but they were all there and the *Gregory Kotovsky* was sunk.

There were two more with them — the third officer and a cabin boy. The officer had wanted to maintain contact with the other boat — Linsky's boat; but Gubin had drawn out his long knife when the man shouted, and had made him realize that it was wiser to be silent.

'We wish to be on our own,' said Gubin. 'You understand?'

The third officer was a very young man. He saw Gubin's knife; he saw Grill's battered face thrust close to his own. He did not understand, but he was silent.

Gubin took the tiller and the others rowed. They rowed until their hands were sore and their backs ached; and the heavy lifeboat moved slowly out into the night — away from Linsky.

11

The Escape

Day came like a punctual guest. One minute it seemed the stars were golden points of flame — the next they had faded, and were gone. The sun came out of the glassy sea like a great disc of fire, and the coolness of night vanished from the air.

They had stopped rowing and stowed the oars. Now they looked at one another as though seeing for the first time who their companions in adversity were. Boyan had a bruise on his right cheek where the lifeboat had struck him, and already his face was dark with a rapid growth of black stubble. He fingered his chin reflectively, as though regretting the lack of a razor.

By tacit consent the leadership had been conceded to Gubin. Hesitantly, the third officer had tried to exert his legal authority, but he had not persisted in the attempt. Seeing with what a crew he had to deal, he realized almost immediately that it was useless. Only from the cabin boy, a frightened wide-eyed youth of fourteen, could he have

248

expected obedience; and what could they hope to accomplish against six resolute and ruthless men?

Gubin asked him what the position of the *Gregory Kotovsky* had been when she sank; and he answered frankly, giving the latitude and longitude as it had been when his last watch finished.

Gubin conferred with his comrades. 'Brazil, I think, we must make our goal. It is nearest.'

He spoke in Russian, and Brett had to translate for Grill's benefit. Grill was in favour of heading north-east, in the direction of Africa, but Brett supported Gubin.

'Best to make for the nearest land; and the wind should help us. Another thing, we shall cut across the lane of shipping coming up from Buenos Aires and Rio.'

Grill still had a fancy for Africa, but he gave in to this reasoning. The mast was set up and the sail was hoisted. Gubin fixed the ration of food and water, and deputed Brett to distribute it twice a day.

'There will be plenty, I think. There are not many of us. But we do not know how long our voyage will be and there is no sense in taking risks.'

Wind came from the south-east, filling the orange-coloured sail. But the lifeboat was heavy, with wide bows; built for the ability to ride a rough sea, and not for speed. It made slow headway.

'Do you think the lifeboats got away from the poop?' Brett asked. He knew that those of the crew who slept aft would have had no chance to make their way forward after the explosion in number four hold. It would have been the after lifeboats or nothing.

Gubin pursed his lips. He answered in Russian. 'Perhaps. I do not know.' It was apparent that he did not care whether they had got away or not. 'We seem to have lost Comrade Linsky. That is the important thing. Linsky will be looking for us; you need not doubt that. We still know too much. Linsky is armed. If that devil gets near us we shall be targets for the little gun. We shall be the dead men that tell no tales.'

Brett had already come to the same conclusion. As they rowed away from the sinking ship they had seen the flash of torch beams and had heard the engine of the motor lifeboat as it hunted for them in the darkness. But the night had been their friend and the hunters had gone off in the wrong direction.

Nevertheless, it was certain that Linsky would not easily abandon the search. In his mind would now be one idea — to destroy in mid-ocean these men who could not now be transported to Russia, these men who held the secret of Grinkov's Tomb.

'I should be glad to see a ship,' Brett said.

Gubin nodded. 'It would be better than Linsky's boat,' he said grimly.

But the sea was empty. There was neither ship nor boat to be seen, only a wide circle of water, shimmering under the tropical sun. And as the day wore on the sun became ever hotter, striking down at them with its bright spears of fire, as they lay unprotected in the open boat. The metal of the gunwale became hot to the touch, like the bar of a stove; they could not bear their hands upon it; and the sail, drawing them slowly westward, seemed to make no impression upon distance, the horizon still as far away as ever.

It was like a dream. Here they lay at the centre of a vast circle, and when they moved the circle moved also. They were always at the hub of their lonely universe and never able to shift one fathom nearer the rim.

The boy sat in the bows for hour after hour, staring at the Englishmen and the Latvians, as though he feared that they might take his life. The third officer had accepted the situation philosophically; he had done what he could to maintain the authority of his rank and could do no more. Now he obeyed orders and asked no questions. There were too many long knives in the boat, and he remembered how the sailor, Tolbukhin, had died. To be ripped open with a knife was not a pleasant death. The third officer gave information or advice when it was demanded of him, and for the rest of the time he remained silent.

Boyan was cheerful. He saw his dreams coming true. He had overcome his fears in order to take part in the plot to sink the *Gregory Kotovsky*, but to the last he had had qualms. Now he felt that the worst was over and his mercurial spirits rose with the rising sun.

He chattered to Brett concerning Brazil, a country about which his ideas were hazy. Brett doubted whether the Armenian had any clear picture of the position of South America on the map of the world; to Boyan, the compass in the boat would have been useless as an aid to navigation, but he was perfectly content to leave such matters to those who understood them. He had unquestioning faith that within a few days at the most they would all be stepping ashore, and that he would at last have his feet planted firmly on the high road to those millions of dollars that constituted his heart's desire.

'From Brazil it is easy to get to America? There are trains, perhaps?'

Brett smiled. He was amused by the steward's peculiar mixture of cunning and simplicity.

'It might be easier to go by sea.'

'By sea?' The idea of trusting himself again to a ship did not seem to appeal to Boyan. 'But it is all one land, is it not? All America. Why go by sea?'

Brett tried to explain the difficulties in the overland route, the extra length of the journey; but Boyan was not persuaded.

'I go by land,' he said, 'not by ship. I have enough of ships. There will be trains.'

'You think you can buy a ticket?'

'If not, I hide under the seat. It will be no trouble.'

All except Boyan and the boy took turns to steer. Boyan was considered useless for the task, and the boy trembled so much when they spoke to him it was obvious he could not be trusted with the tiller. Brett feared that he was suffering from shock. He tried to reassure him, but the boy shrank away like a captured wild animal. He would not accept food when it was offered to him, and his hand shook so violently in taking his ration of water that much of the precious liquid was spilled.

'He is a fool,' Gubin said contemptuously, and shrugged his shoulders.

Brett felt sorry for the boy. He had a

round, innocent face and wide blue eyes; and he was not to blame for the position in which he found himself. But there was no way of helping him. Time would perhaps heal his mind. When he saw that they intended him no harm he might take courage. Meanwhile, it was best to leave him to himself.

Brett, Grill, the three Latvians and the third officer took one-hour spells at the tiller; and for much of the time Gubin and his two compatriots crouched in the waist of the boat and carried on an animated discussion among themselves. In their dirty, unshaven state they looked the perfect picture of conspirators.

Grill, sweating profusely in his blue cotton shirt and trousers, was professionally interested in the boat. He remarked to Brett on certain differences in its construction from that of a British lifeboat. He went from one end of it to the other, examining the equipment with which it was provided, giving little grunts of approval where these were merited, or shaking his head sadly where anything was not up to what he considered the correct standard.

'It ain't too bad,' was his overall verdict.

Time passed slowly; conversation became desultory, flickering up like a blaze fanned by the wind, then dying away again. The boy began to weep silently.

It was shortly after noon when Brett saw a speck far away to the east. He drew the attention of the others to it, pointing.

'There! Over there!'

They shaded their eyes, trying to discern what it might be.

'A ship. Perhaps it is a ship,' Boyan suggested eagerly.

'No,' Gubin said. 'It is not a ship.'

It was too small, too low in the water; it had neither masts nor funnel. An hour later they knew with certainty that it was a boat, and that it was pursuing them.

'It is Linsky,' Gubin said.

No one doubted that he was right. Who else could it be? Boyan's lip trembled.

'He will kill us. He is armed. He will kill us.'

He looked up at the sail and his lips moved as though he were praying for a great wind that should drive them forward, out of reach of the pursuing boat. But the wind did not strengthen, and the lifeboat moved on at the same slow pace, with only a gentle ripple at the bows to show that it was in motion.

Gubin looked at the oars and shook his head. 'It would be of no use. If it is Linsky he will catch us; he has the motor. And if it is

Linsky he will kill us.'

'You think he would shoot us down in cold blood?' Brett said. 'Would even Linsky do that?'

'Cold blood, hot blood; it makes no difference. I do not think Linsky has any hot blood; but he will shoot just the same. He will not dare to let us go; he cannot get us to Siberia now. And he will want revenge, not only for himself, but for his country. Remember that we have sunk a Russian ship, and that Linsky is a great patriot.'

'What's Pete say?' Grill asked, for Gubin had spoken in Russian.

'He says Linsky will shoot us,' Brett answered.

Grill nodded. 'That's what I think, too. It's a pity we didn't take his gun when we had the chance. We could have shot back.'

'Too late to think of that now.'

The other boat drew nearer. Soon they could distinguish the figure of a man standing in the bows, and they could hear the chugging of the engine. The boat held their attention. All except Josef, who was at the tiller, watched with a kind of fascination as the pursuer relentlessly closed the gap. It seemed that they themselves were motionless upon the sea, waiting, waiting.

'Ten more minutes,' Grill said; 'then he'll

be in range. He'll be able to get going with his revolver.'

When the gap had closed to one hundred yards they were able to recognize the figure in the bows as Linsky. He was bare-headed, and the sun glinted on his glasses, so that his eyes, usually so cold and expressionless, seemed in this moment of triumph to flash fire.

'Comrade bloody Linsky,' Grill said; and then was silent. The sound of the engine grew louder. The gap shrank away to fifty yards. Gubin began to count the men in the pursuing boat.

'About fifteen of them, I think. We could not fight it out even if they had no guns.'

'They'll be close enough for Linsky to start firing in a minute,' Brett said. 'We ought to get below the gunwale.'

But nobody moved. The boy continued to weep silently, the big tears rolling down his smooth, hairless cheeks.

The gap was now no more than twenty yards. Linsky shouted. They could hear his squeaky voice above the throb of the engine.

'Drop your sail!'

Gubin gave a hoot of derisive laughter. 'Come and take it down yourself — policeman.'

Boyan said nervously: 'Perhaps we should do as he says. It might be best.'

Gubin sneered. 'Make his work easier? Don't imagine he'll spare you for your pains.'

Linsky shouted again. 'In the name of the Soviet Republic, I order you. Drop your sail, or I shoot.'

'Shoot away then,' Gubin yelled. 'And damnation take you!'

They saw Linsky's right arm come up, the revolver gripped in his hand. They saw him set his legs farther astride to maintain his balance. With his left hand he lent support to his right elbow. They knew that he was about to fire, and yet, somehow, it did not occur to them at that moment to dive below the level of the gunwale and take shelter behind the metal hull. They felt compelled to watch.

Suddenly they heard the crack of Linsky's gun, and the wasp-like buzz of the bullet as it went winging past. Then they were all down in the bottom of the boat. Even Josef was crouching down, holding the tiller with his upstretched hand.

The third officer said: 'You are caught now.' They were the first words he had spoken for almost two hours. Gubin lashed him across the mouth with the back of his hand.

'You keep quiet. We may kill you first.'

The third officer wiped the blood from his lips and said no more. But he looked scared, and his gaze went to Gubin's knife.

The chugging of the other lifeboat's engine sounded very near, and Brett felt an urge to peep over the gunwale to see just where it was. But he knew that Linsky would be waiting for a head to appear; and Linsky might not miss a second time.

Then the engine suddenly choked, spluttered a few times, recovered, spluttered again, and died away into silence.

Brett looked at Grill, crouching beside him, and Grill said: 'Run out of juice, maybe. Lucky for us if they have.'

The mast creaked; wind breathed on the sail; there was a soft, musical gurgle as the bows of the lifeboat rippled the water. After a few minutes Brett lifted his head cautiously and looked over the gunwale.

'All right,' he said. 'We're safe for the present.'

The other lifeboat was wallowing fifty yards astern, and the distance between the two was gradually increasing. They were out of danger from Linsky's revolver, for at that range, with the boat rolling slightly on the swell, he would never have been able to hit his target.

'If that engine died from lack of fuel,' Gubin said, 'we are all right. If it was anything else they may be able to get it started again. I should be glad if it was dark.' But there were four or five hours yet to go before darkness would lend them its welcome cloak and cover their escape. Meanwhile, there was a burst of activity in the other boat. The outline of a spar rose against the sky.

'They are putting up a mast,' Gubin said. 'They will try to catch us under sail.'

Within a few minutes the sail billowed out; but by this time the gap had widened to one hundred and fifty yards. Then the following boat got under way again and settled down once more to the pursuit.

But now there was little to choose between the speeds of pursued and pursuer. The wind remained steady, and there was not much that could be done in the way of skilful sailing to snatch an advantage, where two so evenly matched craft were concerned. The motor lifeboat was the heavier and carried a greater number of passengers, but to compensate for this it possessed a larger spread of canvas.

For a while it seemed to Brett that they were slightly increasing their lead, and he had hopes that they might drop the other boat completely. But an hour passed, and there was no change in the situation. Nevertheless, the fugitives held the advantage, for the sun had passed its zenith, and if only they could hold off the pursuit until darkness came to their aid they would, under cover of night, be able to alter course and escape.

He looked at his watch. It was three o'clock. At six, or a little after, the brief twilight would be rapidly fading out of the western sky. Three more hours and they would be safe — if the engine in the other boat did not come to life again.

'That Linsky will be cursing,' Grill said cheerfully. 'He'll be hopping mad. He nearly had us.'

'He may have us yet,' Brett said.

Grill shook his head. 'Not now. We're safe now.' Gubin took over the tiller from Josef and the slow pursuit went on. Sometimes the gap narrowed a little, sometimes it widened, but it never differed greatly from one hundred and fifty yards.

'Less than a cable's length,' Grill muttered. 'And for all that flaming Linsky can do about it, it might be a hundred miles. I wager he's mad.'

The other sail was always clearly visible, and but for the ripple at the bows, it might have been supposed that both boats were motionless, two fixed points upon the bright blue surface of the sea.

Grill pulled out a big, spotted handkerchief, and wiped the sweat off his face and neck. His shirt was open to the waist, and the tapering picture of the Eiffel Tower was visible in the opening, seeming to stand upon a great roll of flesh, like a lighthouse on a cliff.

'I'd give something for the sight of a ship,' he said. 'Any ship — so long as it wasn't a Russian.'

But the horizon was empty. There was just the wide circle of water with two boats — two boats moving at equal speed across a silent desert that heaved beneath them, as though somewhere, far below, there was life, a breathing, monstrous entity, of which that slight movement on the surface was the only evidence.

At four o'clock Gubin handed the tiller to Nikolai. It should have been the turn of the third officer, but at this critical time they would not trust him. It would have been to his advantage to allow the pursuing boat to catch up. He was a hostage, but a useless one. They could not use his body as a shield; they could not use his life as a counter with which to bargain with Linsky. Comrade Linsky was ruthless; he would not hesitate for a moment to sacrifice the third officer; he was interested in only one thing — the liquidation of those men who possessed the secret of Grinkov's Tomb.

'If we escape,' Gubin said, 'Linsky had better not go back to Russia. It's our lives or his.'

The third officer was more of a liability than an asset — a little more weight in the boat, that was all.

The boy sat motionless, staring. He had ceased to weep, but he was useless also.

'They will catch us,' Boyan said fearfully. 'I am sure they will catch us.'

'Fool!' said Gubin. 'In two hours it will be dark. We shall lose them then. Tomorrow we shall be gone from their sight like a bubble bursting in the air. Without their engine they will never catch us.'

Brett doled out water and biscuits and condensed milk. Still the boy would not eat, but he drank his ration of water thirstily, staring over the rim of the mug with his wide, frightened eyes. Brett wondered how close the kid had been to the explosions in the *Gregory Kotovsky*, how much of his terror was the result of that shock. He remembered his tumbling into the boat just as they were about to push off — a small, wild creature fleeing from the lurid confusion of the sinking ship. Again he felt a surge of pity. What lay ahead for the boy?

If it came to that, what lay ahead for any of them? Death if they were caught by Linsky; the crack of the revolver, the angry hum of the bullet, had left no room for doubt on that score. He looked back and saw the other boat, still about the same distance away. From it came a flash of light as the sun was reflected from some object, perhaps the glass of Linsky's spectacles.

He could imagine that Linsky, too, was counting the hours to sunset, realizing as well as they that he must overtake before darkness hid his quarry in its velvet cloak. The failure of the engine, just when success appeared to be within his grasp, must have maddened him. Brett wondered how much ammunition he had for his revolver. And yet the question was academic; there are more ways of killing a man than shooting, especially in mid-ocean. The odds against the fugitives were too heavy. Their only hope of survival lay in eluding the pursuers.

It was as these thoughts were passing through Brett's mind that the third officer decided to take a hand in the game. Perhaps he, too, had come to the realization that time was slipping away, and that if his compatriots did not overtake before nightfall they would never overtake at all. Whatever the reason that prompted him, he suddenly got to his feet in the stern of the boat and fell heavily against Nikolai, the man at the tiller.

Nikolai, taken completely by surprise, was thrown to one side, and the third officer pushed the tiller hard over, bringing the boat's head round into the wind. The sail flapped uselessly, the boat lost way, and finished in a position broadside on to the pursuing craft.

It was all done in an instant before anyone could move to prevent it. Then Gubin, who had been sitting in the waist of the boat, leaped to his feet with a shout of anger, pulling his long knife from its sheath as he did so. He stumbled over the thwarts in his eagerness to get at the third officer, lifting the knife to plunge it into the man. In a moment more he would have done so, had not Brett seized his arm and struggled with him, holding him back.

He shouted to Grill for assistance. 'Help me. He'll kill that man. Help me, Grill.'

'I'll help you,' Grill said; but instead of seizing Gubin he seized the third officer, and, half-lifting, half-dragging him, tumbled him bodily over the gunwale of the boat.

'Swim to your bloody pal, Linsky,' he yelled. 'Swim for it, you bastard.'

By this time Nikolai had regained control of the tiller and was trying desperately to get the boat under way again. Gubin, seeing what was needed, stopped struggling with Brett and sprang to help with the sail. Slowly, all too slowly, the boat's head came round again and it started to move forward.

But the delay had given the pursuing boat just the chance it needed; the gap was now barely forty yards — and still closing. Again they could see Linsky standing in the bows; again they heard a bullet whine past.

Grill looked over the side and saw that the third officer was hanging on to a loop of the lifeline that encircled the hull of the lifeboat. He slipped his knife from its sheath, leaned over, and slashed at the man's hand.

The man screamed and relaxed his grip. Grill put a fist on his head and thrust him under the bloodstained water.

'Swim, damn you! Swim!'

The third officer came up five yards astern and began to splash, striking out strongly.

'So he can swim,' Grill said. 'Well, that's good. We want them to pick him up.'

An argument seemed to have broken out in the other boat. Across the gap, now only thirty yards wide, they could hear Linsky's high-pitched tones, and another, deeper voice, which Gubin said was that of the *Gregory Kotovsky*'s mate.

It was easy to guess what the argument was about: the mate wanted to stop and pick up the third officer, while Linsky, with victory once again so close, was vehemently insisting that the boat must press on. Brett and his

companions waited anxiously for the out-
come of the argument, for on it might well
depend all their lives.

It was the mate who won. They saw the
boat move away from the line of pursuit to
the point where the third officer was
struggling in the water. Two minutes later he
had been dragged on board, but the gap had
again widened to nearly a hundred yards.

'Why did you hold me back?' Gubin
demanded. 'I would have ripped that devil
open.'

'Better as it is,' Brett said. 'He cost us a bit
of our lead with his tricks, but he has given us
half of it back again.'

Grill was wiping the stain off his knife
before putting it back in the sheath.

'Didn't think he had the guts to do a thing
like that. I thought we had him too much
scared. We oughtn't to have taken a chance
with him. I s'pose the kid ain't likely to try
nothing.'

'Leave him alone,' Brett said. 'He's safe
enough, poor devil. You can see he's shivering
with fright.'

The boy was weeping again, the tears
rolling slowly down his childish face and
leaving little tracks in the grime. Yet he made
no sound. The tears flowed silently, trickling
down towards his chin. He did not try to hide

them; he did not even brush them away. Perhaps he was not aware that he was weeping.

Once again the chase settled into its former routine; the gap neither widening nor closing by more than a few yards. The sun began to slide down the western sky, and the broiling heat of the middle hours of the day moderated as the shadow of the mast and sail lengthened upon the water, stretching out an arm towards the boat that followed. A glitter of flying-fish passed in a curving silver flight, bursting from the sea like leaping jets of mercury, and dropping once more into the element from which they had sprung.

Grill was at the tiller, his heavy, shapeless form huddled in the stern. The remark, when he made it, was spoken so quietly, in so matter-of-fact a way, that for a moment its full significance did not dawn upon Brett.

'The wind's dropping.'

So gradually, almost imperceptibly, had its force decreased that, though all must vaguely have realized it was happening, none of them had really admitted the fact even to himself. Now, as Brett repeated Grill's observation in Russian, they all looked at the sail and then into the face of the wind, and knew that with scarcely an hour to go to sunset their motive power was about to fail them.

'Not now,' Gubin said in a pleading voice. 'Oh, not now. Give us your breath for one hour longer — only one short hour.'

'You cannot command the wind, my friend,' Josef said. 'It is God's will.' He fingered the stubble on his chin. 'Ah, if only I had the little twenty-millimetre cannon that I once used, then I could blow that other boat so full of holes it would sink like a cabbage-strainer. One magazine only would I need.'

'Cry for the moon,' Gubin said. 'It is as likely to come into your hand.'

Brett pointed to Linsky's boat. 'Look there!'

They saw the sail flutter down from the mast; oars splashed into the water. The wind had gone; now it was to become a battle of muscle and sinew.

'The oars!' Gubin cried. 'Man the oars!'

They freed the now useless sail and stowed it away, hastily crumpled.

'You, Anton; take the tiller,' Gubin said. 'We want weight for rowing. Now then, pull till your backs break.' There were only five of them to row, for the boy was useless, and it made the pulling one-sided. But in the other boat ten oars were plying; ten oars drove in pursuit of five. The contest had become as unequal as when the engine had been throbbing; once more the gap began to close.

Brett, dragging at his heavy oar, felt his back muscles begin to ache before the boat had gone a hundred yards; the oar groaned in the rowlock and it seemed as though he were pulling against a dead weight, achieving nothing.

In front of him he could see the sweat pouring down the back of Grill's neck, and the massive shoulders swelling under the soaking shirt. But however the muscles might heave and strain, it was all hopeless: five men could not row against ten and hope to win.

The gap closed to fifty yards, to thirty, to twenty-five.

Linsky balanced himself in the bows of the pursuing boat and took careful aim. The bullet whined past the heads of the rowers and embedded itself in the mast.

'Stop rowing,' Gubin said. 'Get down.'

They obeyed him without question.

Linsky's gun cracked again and a bullet clanged against the hull of the boat, ricocheting away with an angry whine. They needed no stronger urge to haste. The dripping oars clattered on the thwarts and everyone dived for shelter.

There was now no more than twenty yards of clear water between the two boats. In a few moments even that short distance would be cut away, and Linsky would be firing at point blank range.

Brett experienced a cold, sick feeling in the stomach. It was as though they were animals, waiting helplessly to be slaughtered. Then he felt a deep and fiery anger; anger that a creature as contemptible as Linsky should have the power to put such fear into him. His anger drove out the fear. He would not crouch down thus; it was craven, disgusting. He would stand up and face whatever was to come.

He stood up. Then he saw that Gubin was also standing, and that in Gubin's hand was a dark metal object, oval in shape, its surface criss-crossed with grooves. Gubin held it in his right hand, and with his left he drew from it a pin with a ring on the end.

Linsky fired again, and he was so close that Brett could see the expression of hatred on his smooth, pallid face. There was no trace of pity. Brett knew that Linsky would crush out their lives with as little mercy as he would have shown in destroying a nest of vermin.

Gubin took no notice of the whining bullet. He drew back his right arm and calmly and accurately lobbed the metal object into the other boat.

As he did so Linsky's gun fired for the last time, and Gubin, with an expression of

271

almost ludicrous surprise on his square, bony face, clutched at his right shoulder, spun round, and fell back across the centre thwart.

Almost at the same instant Brett heard a sharp, cracking explosion in the other boat. Without a moment's hesitation he flung himself down once more below the level of the gunwale, taking shelter from the blast of the grenade.

Something clanged against the metal hull, and he heard a man screaming.

He raised his head and looked over the gunwale. Then he got to his feet and stood gazing back at the other boat.

No one was rowing any longer; the oars trailed uselessly in the water. Some of the men were moving about in a shocked, dazed manner; two were lying crumpled across the thwarts; and one was holding his arm and screaming. In another moment the screaming dropped to a whimper.

Linsky was lying motionless, with his arms and head dangling over the bows. There was no longer a gun in his hand, and he looked strangely like a rag doll that some child has discarded.

Brett became aware of Gubin's voice — hoarse, urgent, insistent, gasping with pain.

'The oars! Get the oars out! Row!'

He turned and saw that Gubin had struggled up and was sitting on the centre thwart. He was still clutching his right shoulder, and blood was dripping down his hand and staining the shirt. His face was drawn and twisted with the pain; but again he snarled:

'Row, damn you! Row, before they recover.'

Brett took one more look at the other boat and picked up his oar.

12

End of a Journey

The night seemed endless. Brett dozed in brief and fitful snatches, and each time he awoke he found Gubin lying sleepless in the bottom of the boat, his eyes staring up at the star-laden sky, his breath hissing in and out with the pain of his wound.

Linsky's bullet had entered Gubin's chest just below the shoulder, but he had not allowed them to attend to the wound until they had rowed out of sight of the other boat.

'I am all right,' he had repeated vehemently. 'Get away; get away before those devils recover.'

Only when they were alone on the open sea had he given permission for Brett and Nikolai to cease rowing and do what they could for him. When they cut the shirt away they could see the hole under the shoulder, blood still oozing from it. But the bullet had not gone completely through, for there was no hole at the back. It must have come up against a bone and lodged there.

There was a first-aid kit in the equipment

of the lifeboat. They washed the wound with antiseptic and put a pad over it, binding it tightly to stop the bleeding. There was little else they could do.

Then they had started rowing again.

Gubin's lips were pale and there was pain in his eyes; but he made no complaint. All he said was: 'It could have been worse. That Linsky, I think he will never shoot anyone again.'

When Brett went to him at midnight he said: 'I think the stars are very bright tonight.' He spoke in Russian always now, as though too weary to wrestle with another tongue.

'I have not looked at the stars so much since I was a boy,' he said. 'Then I would gaze into the sky, and I would say to myself, 'Hey, Peterkin; there are your jewels'. And I would stretch out my hands and think that I had grasped them; and then I would run to my mother with this so great treasure and I would say to her, 'See, little mother, the lovely jewels that I have brought you.' And then I would open my hands and she would cry, 'Ah, it is so. Ah, my fine, strong boy, to fetch me jewels out of the sky'.'

Gubin smiled sadly. 'My friend, I think you are saying to yourself, what a fool this Peter Gubin is. Never mind. It was a game we used to play; and then we would laugh and dance together, my mother and I. But she is dead now; dead because the Russians took her, took her for a slave; and when they could get no more work out of her they let her die like an animal. And the stars remain; but they are not jewels. No more, no more.'

'Are you warm enough?' Brett asked. He had seen Gubin shiver. 'Take my jacket.' He pulled the jacket off and wrapped it round Gubin's shoulders.

Gubin protested weakly. 'No, no. You need it yourself.'

'I am all right,' Brett said. 'Are you thirsty? Shall I bring you some water?'

Gubin shook his head. 'The water is rationed. I take only my fair share.'

'You will take some now,' Brett insisted. 'But for you we should now all be dead.'

He took some water from one of the beakers with a dipper and brought it to Gubin in a mug. Gubin drank it.

'Is there anything else I can do for you?' Brett asked.

'A cigarette, perhaps. In my pocket you will find a tin with papers and tobacco. If you would roll one for me.'

Brett found the tin and began to roll a cigarette — clumsily, for he was not practised in the art.

Gubin laughed softly. 'I teach you some-time perhaps. I show you the way.'

He took the cigarette and smoked it greedily, as though it were food and drink to him. When he sucked in the smoke the glowing tip of the cigarette was reflected ruddily in his unshaven face.

'How was it that you had a grenade?' Brett asked. Gubin chuckled again. The memory of that last throw seemed to provide him with grim amusement.

'I am a collector of trifles. I say to myself, who knows when this may be useful? I had had it for a long while; and it did come in useful, did it not?'

'Very useful.'

Gubin smoked in silence for a time. Then he said: 'Tomorrow perhaps we see a ship. I will not conceal from you that it would give me pleasure to leave this boat.'

'It will not be long — not long now.'

'I hope you are right. And now you must try to sleep. You need sleep. I can see that you are tired.'

Brett moved towards the bows. He saw that the boy was sleeping peacefully, curled up, with his head pillowed on his arms. Perhaps he would feel better after sleep.

The wind came again with the morning. They hoisted the sail and steered westward.

The sun was their enemy now, beating fiercely down upon them. The sky was a Cyclops' face, and the sun was its eye. But they had no stake with which to blind that eye of fire. The hours dragged by, and there was no ship.

'You'd think,' Grill said, 'that nobody never went to sea. You'd think there wasn't thousands of ships knocking about the oceans of the world, here, there, and everywhere.'

'The sea's too big,' Brett said.

'You're right, it is. Too big, too deep, and too damned salt. It ain't even good to drink.'

By evening Gubin was light-headed. Through the long night he muttered incoherently, twisting and turning under the pain of his wound. The others took turns to watch over him, fearful that he might try to jump from the boat.

The boy seemed to have recovered. Perhaps, seeing the weakness in Gubin, he had forgotten his own weakness. He became eager to help the wounded man. He bathed his brow with a rag dipped in sea-water, and sat for hours with his arm pillowing Gubin's head.

On the third day they heard the sound of an aeroplane, and looked with burning eyes to the sky, in sudden hope. Nikolai was the first to see it. He pointed eagerly to the west.

'There! There!'

It was a single-engined monoplane. It flew over them at a height of about five hundred feet, like a great tropical bird. They stood up in the boat, waving and shouting, not thinking how impossible it was that their feeble shouts should be heard above the roar of the engine.

The plane flew away to the east.

'They didn't see us,' Grill said. He dropped his arms dejectedly. 'They didn't see us.'

But the plane turned and came back, almost skimming the water. It dipped its wings in salutation, and they could see the stars painted on them. Then it climbed rapidly and flew back towards the west.

Two hours later a cruiser of the United States Navy had taken them into its care.

★　★　★

The captain of the cruiser was at first inclined to be sceptical of the story that Brett related to him. He was a tough-looking, sunburnt man of about forty, with a keen, quizzical eye and a humorous twist of the lip. He was obviously not one to be taken in by fairy stories; he had heard so many.

Brett started at the beginning, the night when the *Silver Tassie* was rammed in the fog in the Barents Sea. From there he went on in chronological order to the interrogation by Linsky, to the re-fuelling in mid-ocean, and the arrival at Grinkov's Tomb.

When he described the hidden anchorage and the submarine pens cut out of the rock the captain's eyebrows rose slightly.

'How many submarines did you see?'

'We saw twelve, but there may have been many more in the pens.'

'I see. Well, go on.'

Brett continued his story. He told how he and Grill had come to the realization that they would never be allowed by the Russians to give away such information, that if they reached Russia they would never come out of that country alive, and that somehow they must escape from the *Gregory Kotovsky*.

'And then?'

'Gubin — the man who is wounded — he is a Latvian — he had reasons for escaping also. He suggested sinking the ship and getting away in the confusion.'

'Ah! And how did he propose doing that?'

'By blowing holes in the hull with explosives he had taken from the cargo.'

'That was a desperate plan.'

'We were in a desperate situation. I think, sir, you would have been desperate too in our place.'

'Maybe.' The captain's voice was non-committal. He did not say that he disbelieved, but he did not give the impression that he was convinced.

Brett went on to describe the death of Captain Govorov, the release of Josef from his cell, and the blowing up of the ship; the long pursuit in the boats and the final throw of Gubin's hand-grenade.

The captain listened to it all very patiently, but before he left Brett he said: 'I think that what you need is a good long sleep. You've had a pretty tough time.'

It was as much as to say that in his opinion Brett's ordeal in the lifeboat had coloured his imagination.

An hour later he returned, and this time when he spoke there was no longer the doubtful, half-humorous expression on his face.

'I have been checking up,' he said. 'The *Silver Tassie* — that was the name of the ship you said you were sailing to Russia in, wasn't it?'

Brett nodded.

'The *Silver Tassie* was lost, with all hands, in fog on a voyage to Archangel. A radio signal was picked up, saying that she had been rammed and was sinking rapidly. After that nothing more was heard.'

'Not all hands. Two of us escaped. I am sorry to hear that all the others were drowned, though I was afraid that it must be so.'

'In addition,' said the captain, 'a report has just come through that ten Russians, one badly wounded, have been rescued by a Brazilian steamer. They were drifting in a lifeboat some fifty miles east of the position in which we found you.'

'So you believe me now?'

The captain did not say whether he believed or not. He simply added: 'I have been in touch with the Navy Department. We have orders to proceed to Baltimore with all speed.'

13

End of a Story

Brett Manning, junior partner in the firm of Josiah Manning, Son, and Company Limited, handed a letter that he had been reading across the breakfast table to his wife.

'Perhaps you'd like to read this, Jennie. It's from that little Armenian I told you about — Anton Boyan.'

Jennifer Manning took the letter. 'Is he a millionaire yet?'

'Well, not exactly, darling; but on the way.'

'Mr Manning dear sir,' the letter began.

Now that I have learn some of the English language, I write to tell you how glad I am that I come to this great country of America. Also I thank you again for your so much help to get me here. I work now in a garage. It is near New York which is a fine city and beat Erivan like nobody's business. We do much trade and take many many dollars, all crisp and crackling like you say.

I get on with my boss, Joe, very well thank you. He have very pretty daughter who is twenty-two years old and call me Anton. I call her Honey and sometimes Baby, though she is not small and know more than any baby whatever. One day I marry her and when Joe die I think maybe I take the garage. Joe is forty-five and big, strong, healthy man, but he drive very fast cars, so who know what may happen?

I must tell you, one week ago Joe say to me that there is three men ask to see me. Me? I say. I think it must be the cops, though I do nothing the cops should worry about. But it is not the cops, it is those three sailors, Peter Gubin, Josef Slowacki, and Nikolai Vilhelms. They so glad to see me and I say I am glad to see them, too. They have big car and they say fill her up with gas, Anton, and then they laugh most much ha-ha.

They not sailors now. They American citizens like me and they work in a glue factory and make good money. I tell them I write to you and they say send their good wishes, so that is what I do. I ask them about the boy and they say he go back to Russia. He have no sense, that boy. Then they say good luck, Anton, and they start the big car and drive off like hell.

I hope you are very well and that you marry that pretty girl you so often tell me about. I use a dictionary what Joe lend me, so I spell this letter damn good.

Best wishes from
ANTON BOYAN

Jennifer pushed the letter back across the table.

'Who was the pretty girl you told him about?'

'Give you three guesses,' Brett said.

He was pleased to have received the letter. He had been wondering about Boyan and Gubin and the others. It was now nearly six months since he and Grill had left America, and in all that time he had been ignorant of what had happened to his fellow fugitives from the *Gregory Kotovsky*. Well, it seemed that they had fallen on their feet, just as he had done.

Brett was happy. Who could be happier? Married to a girl like Jennifer, junior partner in a thriving firm of timber merchants, there was nothing more that he desired. And for his happiness he owed so much to Gubin and Boyan, to Josef and Nikolai; he was glad to hear that they were doing well.

As for Grill, he was away again. For a while he had accepted work in the timber yard, but soon the wanderlust had got into him again, and he had sailed away in a ship bound for

Australia. Brett had had a card from Singapore, and that was the last he had heard of Grill. He would not be surprised if Grill jumped ship in Australia and wandered about that continent. No doubt he would hear some time.

He glanced at the morning paper and a headline caught his eye: 'Russia Accuses US'.

With suddenly awakened interest he read on.

The Soviet Union has accused the United States of exploding a nuclear weapon in the Southern Ocean. She alleges that this has caused a fall-out of radio-active dust likely to endanger whaling-fleets in the vicinity. It is claimed that a small uninhabited island, known as Grinkov's Tomb, has been almost completely destroyed. The United States' answer to this accusation is a complete denial.

Note: Grinkov's Tomb has for years been avoided by shipping because of a dangerous reef, on which several ships have been wrecked.

'Well, well, well,' Brett said.

'Something interesting?' Jennifer asked.

Brett put down the paper and attacked his breakfast. 'Nothing for us to worry about. Just the end of a story.'

Books by James Pattinson Published by The House of Ulverscroft:

WILD JUSTICE
THE WHEEL OF FORTUNE
ACROSS THE NARROW SEAS
CONTACT MR. DELGADO
LADY FROM ARGENTINA
SOLDIER, SAIL NORTH
THE TELEPHONE MURDERS
SQUEAKY CLEAN
A WIND ON THE HEATH
ONE-WAY TICKET
AWAY WITH MURDER
LAST IN CONVOY
THE ANTWERP APPOINTMENT
THE HONEYMOON CAPER
STEEL
THE DEADLY SHORE
THE MURMANSK ASSIGNMENT
FLIGHT TO THE SEA
DEATH OF A GO-BETWEEN
DANGEROUS ENCHANTMENT
THE PETRONOV PLAN
THE SPOILERS
HOMECOMING
SOME JOB
BAVARIAN SUNSET
THE LIBERATORS
STRIDE

FINAL RUN
THE WILD ONE
DEAD OF WINTER
SPECIAL DELIVERY
SKELETON ISLAND
BUSMAN'S HOLIDAY
A PASSAGE OF ARMS
OLD PALS ACT
ON DESPERATE SEAS
THE SPAYDE CONSPIRACY
CRANE

We do hope that you have enjoyed reading this large print book.

Did you know that all of our titles are available for purchase?

We publish a wide range of high quality large print books including:
Romances, Mysteries, Classics
General Fiction
Non Fiction and Westerns

Special interest titles available in large print are:
The Little Oxford Dictionary
Music Book
Song Book
Hymn Book
Service Book

Also available from us courtesy of Oxford University Press:
Young Readers' Dictionary
(large print edition)
Young Readers' Thesaurus
(large print edition)

For further information or a free brochure, please contact us at:
Ulverscroft Large Print Books Ltd.,
The Green, Bradgate Road, Anstey,
Leicester, LE7 7FU, England.
Tel: (00 44) **0116 236 4325**
Fax: (00 44) **0116 234 0205**

STRANGER IN THE PLACE

Anne Doughty

Elizabeth Stewart, a Belfast student and only daughter of hardline Protestant parents, sets out on a study visit to the remote west coast of Ireland. Delighted as she is by the beauty of her new surroundings and the small community which welcomes her, she soon discovers she has more to learn than the details of the old country way of life. She comes to reappraise so much that is slighted and dismissed by her family — not least in regard to herself. But it is her relationship with a much older, Catholic man, Patrick Delargy, which compels her to decide what kind of life she really wants.